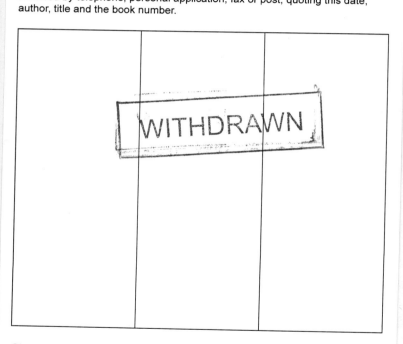

*For anyone who feels that the world
is a confusing place*

Chapter 1

My sister Kaydee is the most beautiful person in the world. She doesn't believe it, and she hates me telling her. She says, 'Oh, stop it, Darby, I'm totally not. My nose is too big and my thighs are too fat, and I have spots which are just ugh.' And if I tell her again that she's beautiful, she gets cross and won't speak to me.

It's funny, because I like it if someone tells me I'm beautiful. Mum tells me I'm beautiful, and it makes me feel warm and happy, not cross and upset.

When Kaydee's friend Lissa met me for the first time, she said to Kaydee, 'What's wrong with your sister then?' and Kaydee went all pink and said, 'Nothing's wrong with her. Don't say that. She's got Down's syndrome. It makes her look a bit different from other people.'

Lissa sort of wrinkled up her nose. I wrinkled up my nose too because the way she spoke was stinky. And actually Lissa was kind of stinky too with a lot of perfume. So I said, 'You smell,' and Kaydee gasped and said, 'Darby! That's rude!' and Lissa said, 'It's body spray. You should try it sometime. Not that I'm saying you *need* it . . .'

That confused me, because I couldn't work out what she meant. Did I need it, or didn't I? Sometimes people say one thing and mean another, which makes me mixed up.

Kaydee took a breath and said, 'Lissa, Darby is my sister and I love her more than anything. Darby, Lissa is my friend and I don't want you to be horrible to her. All right?'

'Well, *she* can't be horrible to *me*,' I said firmly.

Kaydee nodded. 'She won't be. I promise.'

I live with Kaydee and my mum and my dad and my brother on a strawberry farm. People always look interested when I tell them that. Not many people live on a strawberry farm. 'How lovely!' they say. 'Being able to eat strawberries all the time!'

No one wants to eat strawberries *all* the time. The only thing I want to eat all the time is chocolate.

My brother Olly is actually my stepbrother, and he can't eat strawberries. He's fifteen and he's allergic. If he eats a strawberry, he gets a rash all over and then he can't breathe. He's got a special injection that looks like a pen, in case it happens. It's kept in the kitchen drawer and I am definitely not allowed to touch it.

Kaydee is sixteen. I'm twelve. Mum is thirty-six, and my dad Paul, who is actually my stepdad, is forty-six. If you add up all our ages, you get a big number. If you added in all the ages of all the people who also work on the farm, you'd get an even bigger number. And if you added in the ages of the two dogs and the cat . . . well, you'd need a calculator.

Today is Friday, but it's the holidays so I'm not at school. Instead, Kaydee and I are sitting at the kitchen table. She is on her phone. I am doing some painting by numbers. It's where you have a black-and-white drawing and you have to colour it in, and little numbers tell you which colour to put where. I looooove painting by numbers. Almost as much as I love music. In fact, the world is perfect right now, because I have my earphones in and I am listening to my favourite songs *while* I paint.

I remember . . .

. . . years ago when my stepdad asked me what my favourite songs were. I played him lots, and then he said, 'Would you like to hear one of my favourites?' It was by a boy band from the last century and it was about a woman who kept her face in a jar by the door. Dad said, 'Listen, Darby, this is such a clever song.'

I thought it was very weird. I wouldn't want to keep taking my face off and putting it on again. It would be really annoying. And the song wasn't the sort you could dance to.

Dad said, 'Don't you think it's clever, Darby?'

I didn't think it was clever. But I like Dad and I didn't want to hurt his feelings, so I shrugged and said, 'Yeah.'

The tune from the chorus stayed in my head for weeks though.

Chapter 2

There is one other thing that is making me perfectly happy, and that is the thought of the chocolate hunt. On Sunday, in two days' time, it is Easter, and at Easter we do a chocolate egg hunt. Mum buys four packets of small chocolates wrapped in coloured foil and she hides the chocolates in the garden, in plants and between the stones and places like that. The rest of us go around trying to find them. If you find one, you get to put it in your basket. We have special baskets that are years old. We always use the same ones. Mine is green. Kaydee laughs and makes fun of the chocolate hunt but she still takes part. Even Olly, who pretends nothing is fun apart from video games, turns up for it.

I love the chocolate hunt. I look forward to it for months. 'Is it today?' I ask Mum a thousand times. 'Is it today? Is it tomorrow?'

Just as I am thinking about Mum, she comes into the kitchen. She's quite short, like me, and she has pale soft hair and a pale soft face, with light brown eyes. She's wearing jeans and a blue shirt and a big fleece. She starts talking but I can't hear her because music is playing in my ears. She makes the sign to me to remove my earphones.

'Darby, have you brushed your teeth?' she asks.

'Yes,' I say, even though I haven't. Brushing teeth is very boring. And it means going up the stairs. I'm sitting down now.

Mum runs her hand through her hair, which is all messy. 'I've been checking the tunnels,' she says, and her forehead creases up like when you fold paper to make a fan.

She means the polytunnels. Polytunnels are made of big metal hoops, with plastic stretched over them. Our farm has three sites. The one we live on has four big greenhouses, and the other two sites (which are about ten minutes' drive away) have polytunnels. All of them are packed with strawberry plants. At this time of year there are lots of green fruits on them, slowly ripening.

'Why?' asks Kaydee. It isn't usually Mum's job to check the tunnels. That's what Dad does with

Juris, one of our managers. Juris is actually from Latvia, which is one of the Baltic States, which always makes me think of baldness, but Juris has lots of black hair so he's not in the least bald, not one tiny bit.

'Wind's getting up,' Mum says, and Kaydee and I know not to ask any more. Farmers are obsessed with wind. This always makes me giggle, because 'wind' is also about farts, but Dad says it's not a laughing matter. High wind can knock out electricity lines and pull apart plastic sheeting. It can also suck out glass from windows if it's strong enough. Like a huge vacuum cleaner in the sky.

Mum goes to the sink and fills the kettle with water. The sink is big and square and ceramic. The tap is a bit drippy if you don't turn it off properly. To the right of the sink is the draining board, and against the wall to the left is the cooker, big and black and hot all the time because it's an oil-fired Aga and you can dry your clothes on it double-quick. I like leaning against the Aga.

When Mum has filled the kettle, she stands and stares out of the window for a moment. Then Kaydee says, 'Er, Mum? You forgot to switch the kettle on.'

'Oh!' Mum blinks. 'Sorry. Don't know where my head is this morning.'

I think I've probably been paying attention for long enough, so I put my earphones back in. But before the next song starts up, I hear Mum say, 'Could be a tornado on the way.'

Tornadoes are bad. I used to get tornadoes confused with tomatoes. I knew they were different things but sometimes I get words mixed up. A tornado can whip through our farm and blow out all the glass from one of our huge greenhouses without touching anything else. A tomato can't do that.

Tornadoes make everyone around here stressed (unlike tomatoes, which just make *me* stressed). When people are stressed they shout at each other. I don't like people shouting. I turn up the volume in case Mum is about to start.

And then it occurs to me that if people are stressed, and a tornado is blowing all over the place, then the chocolate hunt is in danger.

So I take out my earphones and say, 'We're still doing the chocolate hunt, right?'

Mum is in the middle of a sentence but I don't know what she was saying. It's very important that she hears me. 'I still want to do the chocolate hunt,' I say, more loudly.

'Darby.' Mum sounds annoyed. 'I'm in the middle of talking to Kaydee. I've told you about interrupting. You need to wait until there's a break in conversation.'

'Yes, I know,' I say, 'but the chocolate hunt.'

'You and your chocolate hunt!' Kaydee exclaims. 'There are other things going on, you know, Darby. Mum's really worried about the wind. The forecast is really bad.'

'But –'

'Darby,' Mum says in that tone of voice that lets me know she's mad at me, 'I don't know if the chocolate hunt will go ahead or not. It depends entirely on the wind and the state of affairs on Sunday.'

I stare at her. 'I want to do it,' I say, in case she hasn't quite understood.

'I will do everything I can to make sure it happens,' Mum says, and I breathe a sigh of relief. It's going to be OK.

I remember . . .

. . . a chocolate hunt one year where Mum forgot to shut the back door. We were all inside waiting because Olly was in the loo and we couldn't start without him. But the chocolate was all out in the garden, and the dogs found it first.

Our dogs now are called Marmite and Bramble, but back then we didn't have Marmite; we had another dog called Lolly. Lolly was a really good sniffer dog, and she sniffed around the garden and ate a *lot* of chocolate, maybe twenty or thirty little ones, in their foil wrappers. When we got outside and saw what was happening, Mum went crazy. She shouted at the dogs and they put their tails between their legs and looked all sorry, and then Mum and Dad put both dogs in the Land Rover and drove them to the vet. Chocolate is poisonous to dogs, and tin foil isn't something anyone should eat. The vet did some things to the dogs, and Bramble was

OK. I think maybe he hadn't eaten as much as Lolly. Lolly died.

I was very sad that Lolly died. But I was also sad that most of the chocolate had gone. I only found six chocolates in the garden, and one of them had teeth marks in it.

Kaydee's phone beeps her text noise, and she taps the screen and reads the message, and her face goes all smiley. I know what that means.

'She's on her way,' says Kaydee.

Lissa is coming to stay this weekend. She's going to stay three whole nights. Which means she'll be here for the chocolate hunt. She's nicer to me now than she was at the beginning, but I'd still rather she wasn't here for my favourite thing. And I'm worried about the baskets. You see, we have the right number of baskets for one each – me, Olly, Kaydee and Dad (Mum doesn't have one, obviously, because she sets out the chocolate). Four baskets. But if there are *five* people doing the hunt, we won't have enough.

I sigh.

'What's the matter?' Kaydee asks me.

I shrug. 'Nothing.'

'Darby, Lissa's my friend, so you could at least try to be nice to her.'

'I am nice!' I say.

'You always make a face when I mention her,' Kaydee tells me.

'I don't,' I retort. 'This *is* my face.' I stick out my tongue.

Kaydee sticks out her tongue in response. Hers

is very thin and pointy and she can touch her nose with it. I can't do that. Mum says Kaydee gets her tongue from our dad, Hayden. We haven't seen him for years so I can't ask him to stick out his tongue to check for myself.

'Don't be childish,' Mum says, and then turns to Kaydee. 'Do I need to come up and sort your room?'

'I've done it,' says Kaydee. 'Sheets all changed and everything.'

Something inside me feels sore. Sometimes, if I have a bad dream or I just want some company, I get up in the night and go up the steep stairs to Kaydee's room. I burrow under her duvet and snuggle up with her, and she drapes a toasty-warm arm around me and mutters, 'All right, Darby?' and goes back to sleep. This is the first time Lissa has stayed over and I hadn't thought about where she would be sleeping. I don't want her sharing a bed with Kaydee.

'What if I need to come into your bed?' I ask Kaydee.

She pulls a funny face. 'Well, you can't. Lissa will be there.'

'But what if I have a bad dream?' I say.

'You'll have to go and see Mum,' Kaydee tells me.

'I'd rather you didn't,' Mum says, smiling but in a voice that tells me she means it. 'You sleep in the weirdest positions.'

It's true. I do sleep in funny positions, like curled up at the bottom of my bed right under the duvet, or half on the bedside table, my arm twisted round the lamp. I don't do it on purpose; it's just what's comfortable at the time. I like sleeping. But I don't want to be on my own if I'm scared. I'm worried now, so I look scowly.

Mum looks out of the window again. 'This wind . . .' She drinks some coffee. 'We just have to hope.'

I stop listening to her and go back to my painting. Number four: brown. For the tree trunks and the girl's hair . . . My mouth moves by itself. I do this thing where I talk to myself. It's like a conversation with myself, but if anyone asks me what it's about, I can't tell them. Sometimes I'm just repeating a word I like. Or what other people have just said. Sometimes the words aren't even proper words. When I do it, I stop listening to what's going on around me. It's kind of nice. Like an off switch for the world.

After a while, Kaydee goes out of the kitchen and Mum does too. I finish my painting. I am really pleased with it. I've hardly gone over the lines at all, and I only made a mistake with the colour twice.

I look around to show it to someone, but the kitchen is empty, apart from Pike, the black cat, who has padded in and is standing on the end of the table. He's probably hoping for food. He's not supposed to be on the table, but right now he's the only one here, so I encourage him over and show him my painting. 'Look,' I say.

Pike sniffs at it, but it's not food so he doesn't care. He nudges at my hand. I pick him up and squidge him in a proper cuddle. His black fur is so soft, and dark as midnight. He wriggles away and jumps down to the floor. He doesn't like being squidged.

I look around the kitchen and sigh. Something feels wrong. I don't know what it is, and I don't like the feeling.

Luckily I know what to do when I have feelings I don't like.

It's time to find some music.

Chapter 3

My room is on the first floor at the end of the house. You go up the stairs from the hall, turn left and there's Olly's bedroom. Next to him is Mum and Dad's room. On the left of that is the bathroom, and left of *that* is my bedroom. There are a lot of lefts in our house. Unless you're facing the other way, when there would be a lot of rights. I have one bed, two windows and lots of my things. And no one is allowed in my room except Kaydee and Mum.

And me of course. Because that would be silly, if I couldn't go in my own room.

I have lots of posters of pop bands and of dolphins. I like dolphins and one day I want to swim with them. It won't matter that I can't swim very well because the dolphins will help me.

I have speakers that connect to my iPod, so I

can listen to music. I also have a laptop, and I love watching music videos online. I practise the moves so that I can do them along with the dancers on the screen. That's what I'm doing now. Dancing is the only exercise I like. I'm in a dance group at school and we dance to all our favourite songs.

'Darby!' yells Olly from his room. 'Turn it down!'

I don't want to turn it down, so I ignore him. And then there are more footsteps on the stairs, and I hear Kaydee's voice, and so I pause the video and open my bedroom door and come out onto the landing.

She's there with Lissa. Today, Lissa has purple streaks in her hair and purple nail varnish. Purple is her favourite colour. Once she and Kaydee went out to a party and Lissa wore all purple clothes, and she even had purple lipstick and purple boots.

She looked like a giant grape.

When she's not dressing like a grape, Lissa has light brown hair and brown eyes and lots of freckles, which she hates. Kaydee teases her about them and Lissa punches Kaydee on the arm. It's a joke, but she always does it too hard and Kaydee winces and then Lissa apologises and they make up. It happens every time. Lissa also has spots, like

Kaydee, but she paints over them with foundation, and you can only tell they're there because they look like tiny mountains on her forehead and chin.

'Aren't you going to say hello?' asks Kaydee. I realise I've been staring at Lissa's face for several moments, not saying anything.

'Hi, Lissa,' I say.

'Hi, Darby,' she says back, and she smiles at me. 'You OK?'

But this is one of those questions I'm not supposed to reply to, because as soon as she's said it, she turns and goes up the narrow flight of stairs to Kaydee's room, which is where the loft used to be before Mum and Dad had it converted. Kaydee's bedroom is the biggest one of the whole house, but you can't stand up in all of it, and half of it is divided off into 'storage', which basically means 'everything we don't know what to do with so we'll dump it up here'. Kaydee moans about it, but I know it's pretend because she loves being up there away from everyone.

I love it up there too. So, without thinking, I follow her and Lissa up the stairs.

'Oh.' Lissa sees me as I emerge. 'Um . . .'

Lissa's purple suitcase is on Kaydee's bed. Kaydee

unzips it and flings it open. 'You might as well unpack properly since you're here for three nights! I cleared a drawer for you.'

'You did?' Lissa looks pleased. 'That's . . . really sweet of you.'

Kaydee starts taking out clothes from Lissa's case. 'This is gorgeous!' she says, holding up a purple top.

I reach across and pull out something stringy and pink, with a bit of lace on it. 'What's this?'

Lissa snatches it out of my hand. 'Don't touch my stuff! That's personal.'

Kaydee says, 'Don't be mad at her. She didn't mean to.'

My eyes sting behind my glasses and I blink lots. 'Sorry,' I say.

'Does she *have* to be up here?' Lissa says to Kaydee.

Kaydee looks at her for a moment and then she turns to me. 'Darby, would you mind going back to your room for a bit? Lissa and I haven't seen each other for a while. We've got lots to catch up on.'

'You saw each other last week,' I object. 'And you're always texting each other.'

'Darby . . .' Kaydee says again, and her voice is not so friendly, 'I'm asking nicely.'

I glance at Lissa. Her black-lined eyes are narrowed and looking at me very hard.

'Fine,' I say. 'I didn't want to be up here anyway in your stupid room with your stupid friend.' I turn and start down the stairs. When I get to the landing below, I hear laughter break out above me.

'Oh, I'm sorry,' I hear Kaydee say. 'She just doesn't . . . you know. Some things she just doesn't get.'

I get it, I think. You like your friend Lissa more than me. I go to my room and SLAM MY DOOR REALLY LOUD.

Chapter 4

My room is tidy because I like things to be in the right places. I don't have clothes all over the floor, like Olly, or thirty make-up and perfume bottles on my dressing table, like Kaydee. I have a dark blue carpet, which was really expensive and Mum didn't want me to have it. 'It won't wear well,' she said, but I insisted. It's soft and fluffy and I like walking on it in bare feet. It makes me feel warm and tingly.

The walls are whitish, and I have a big wardrobe that looks like it could have come from the books about Narnia. It doesn't lead into another world though. I've checked. I also have a chest of drawers. On top of the drawers is a set of shelves, where I keep my books and useful things. I like books but I'd rather listen to music or watch videos on my laptop.

I have just picked up my iPod when the door is

flung open again. Olly is standing there, looking very cross. Olly is quite short for his age, like me. He has thick black hair that he spends ages on, making it look like he just got out of bed. (When he *has* actually just got out of bed, his hair is all flat on one side and not cool at all.) He has a pointy nose and blue-grey eyes and he acts like everything is an effort. 'Darby,' he says, 'are you *trying* to ruin my career?'

Olly plays computer games all the time. He says he wants to make it as a gamer. I don't know how this is actually a job, but he says it is and he knows more about computers than anyone else in our family.

I glare at him. I feel all hot and tight on the inside. 'What are you talking about?' I ask.

'I was in a four-way fight,' says Olly, 'and your door slamming made me lose my concentration and I *died*.'

He means died in the game of course. Not died for real. Because then he wouldn't be talking to me.

'The world doesn't revolve around you,' I say crossly, and fling myself on my bed, putting in my earphones. I don't know quite what it means, but Mum says it when she's annoyed with me.

'It doesn't revolve around you either,' says Olly, pulling one of my earphones out. 'Just because you're *special* doesn't mean you get to ruin my life.'

I hate it when he calls me special. When Mum and Dad first got together, Olly used to call me Moonface behind their backs. Then one day he got into BIG trouble for it, and he stopped doing it. But I haven't forgotten. I have a *really* good memory.

'Go away,' I say to him, and I pull on the other end of the earphone.

'Did you have an argument with Kaydee?' Olly's voice suddenly goes all babyish. 'Ahh, did poor Darby-warby have an argument with Kaydee-waydee?'

'Go *away*,' I say. 'I didn't have an argument. It was Lissa.'

'Lissa?' Olly lets go of the earphone in surprise. 'Is she here?'

'You don't listen to anything,' I tell him. 'Of course she's here. She's staying for the weekend.'

'For the *weekend*?' He looks cross. 'Why so long?'

'*I* don't know,' I say. 'Go away.'

And this time he does. I'm not surprised Olly didn't know that Lissa was coming. He doesn't listen to half the stuff Mum says, or any of us say for that matter. The only person he ever really listens to is Kaydee.

I flick through my music collection and find one that I can turn up very, very loud. And then I get off the bed and make up a dance routine to it.

Chapter 5

When I come down later, it's because I'm feeling hungry. But there's no one downstairs at all. Mum's study, to the right of the kitchen, is empty. Mum and Dad must be out on the site. I look out of the kitchen window and see the trees blowing about all over the place. The wind does look bad.

But I'm hungry. And I'm not allowed to help myself to food from the fridge or the cupboards. Mum's very strict about that. If I want to have something to eat, I'm going to have to find her.

I go through the hall to the utility room and turn the handle of the back door. The wind almost blows the door into my face, and for a moment I think maybe I'll just go back to my room. But my tummy rumbles, so I go out, leaving the door open behind me.

You can see the biggest greenhouse from our

kitchen window. The path from the back door is quite short, and then you're on the track that goes all the way around the site. You have to watch out because there's often a tractor or a Land Rover or something driving on it. Or a minibus. In the summer we have lots of people come and work on the farm, picking the fruit, and they all have to be driven from site to site wherever they're needed. But it's not summer yet so it's still just the people who are here all year. Juris and his family live in a proper house, but most of the others live in caravans right here. We have loads of empty caravans, ready for the summer fruit pickers.

The little tree at the end of the path is bending over so far it's almost snapping in two. My hair is blowing in my face, and my trousers are flapping around my legs. It's horrible. But I'm getting hungrier by the minute, so I set off.

I walk round the end of greenhouse number one and tug open the sliding door. Inside, it's suddenly very quiet, and my hair falls down straight instead of sideways into my eyes. 'Mum!' I call.

I walk down the middle of the greenhouse. To my left and right are rows and rows of strawberry plants in special earth bags. They're not on the ground – they're at about the same height as my head, on metal tables. In the ceiling are vents, so that air moves around the plants while they're growing. There aren't any sprinklers because the plants get their water from pipes that go into the bags.

It's all very, very technical and boring and the green fruits aren't ripe yet (although they will be in a couple of weeks), so I don't even glance at the plants as I walk down the middle of the greenhouse. 'Mum!' I call again.

At the other end, I pull open the sliding door and step out into the blowing wind again. It's like being shoved by lots of people, so that it's hard to stand up. But I still haven't found Mum, so I keep going towards the site office. I know I'll find people in there.

The site office is in a big metal box called a Portakabin. It's full to bursting with paper and files and computers and random stuff in boxes. Juris is in there with Dad, and they are looking at the computer screen. Dad turns round as I come in. 'Darby,' he says, 'you all right?'

'I'm hungry,' I say.

'Well, go and make yourself a sandwich.'

'I can't,' I say. 'I need to find Mum.'

'I don't know where she is right now,' he says, and then he turns back to the computer screen, which is showing a swirly yellow and green thing and lots of lines and little numbers. 'We should move the vans to the end of the tunnels,' he says to Juris.

Juris nods, his head bouncing like a ball. 'The easterly end.'

Dad says, 'Yes, going by the projected route. Anything to ease the pressure on the plastic. We shouldn't have skinned them so early.'

I wait, but they carry on talking in fast voices and I lose track of what they're saying.

I go into each of the other three greenhouses – wind blowing, struggling against it; sudden quiet, tangled hair – but Mum isn't there, and no one can help me. When I reach the road, I stop for a moment. She could be at one of the other sites, I suppose, so I turn left and start walking.

It's very difficult to walk in this wind. I keep getting pushed over by sudden gusts and stumbling into the road. A car coming past honks its horn as it swerves around me. I jump back onto the grass verge, but it's so difficult to stay upright. As

I walk, I grumble to myself about sandwiches and mums and walking.

At a fork in the road, I turn right. I know exactly where I'm going. I don't remember how far the site is, but I'll recognise it when I get there. I trip on a lumpy bit of ground and feel pain shoot up my leg. 'Ow!' I bend down and rub my ankle, just as a gust of wind shoves me into a patch of nettles. 'OW!'

I get up. My ankle isn't too bad after the initial shock, but my hand is all stung from the nettles. Now I'm hungry *and* in pain *and* grumbly. But I still haven't found Mum, so I keep going.

A branch whips me in the face. There's so much NOISE around, from the trees rustling and cracking. I don't like it. I put my hands over my ears, wincing as the stinging hurts even more, and keep walking.

Then someone grabs my shoulder.

Chapter 6

I *totally* freak out, like jump a metre in the air and shriek from fright. And then I turn and see Mum standing next to me, looking really cross. 'Mum!' I say, relieved and delighted.

'Darby,' she calls over the wind, 'what on earth are you doing out here?'

'I'm hungry,' I yell back. 'I was coming to find you.'

'You're *two miles* from home,' she shouts. 'Get in the car.'

I hadn't heard the engine because of all the wind noise, and because I had my hands over my ears. I'm very glad to climb into the car and shut the door. The air in here is still and quiet. My ears feel numb, like after you've been to a festival where they play really loud music. I look down at my hand. It's red and white with the bumpy stings.

Mum gets into the driver's seat. 'Put your belt on,' she says sharply. 'Did you even *tell* anyone where you were going?'

I put on my belt and pretend I haven't heard her. Now that I'm in the car, of course I remember I'm not supposed to leave our site without asking or letting people know. But I didn't remember that back at home.

'You *have* to stop wandering off on your own, Darby,' Mum says as she drives home. 'It's so dangerous. What if you'd fallen in a ditch and couldn't get up? How would we know you needed help?'

I don't like it when people are angry with me. It makes me feel bad, so I get grumpy. 'I didn't fall in a ditch.' I don't dare tell her about my ankle or my stinging hand.

'That's not the *point*, Darby.' Mum uses my name extra often when she's cross. She is stressed, I can tell. Her hair is all blown about like mine, and her body is tight and crunched up, her shoulders stiff.

I don't say any more, but we're nearly back home anyway. I *have* walked a long way. Still, I found Mum, so that's all right.

We get back to the house and Mum jumps out. 'I have to go to the site office,' she says. 'Go into the house and stay there. I'll be there in a minute.'

'But I'm hungry!' I say.

'Then make yourself a sandwich. Or have an apple. Honestly, Darby, you're twelve years old, you can make your own snack.' Then she is gone.

I can't believe it. She's always told me *not* to make a snack without asking. I followed the rules! And now she's telling me off! How is that fair?!

I stomp into the house and go straight to the kitchen. I knock the lid off the bread bin and it clatters onto the side. I grab two slices of bread and a knife from the drawer, and I butter the bread. I'm not very neat but it's fine. And then I go to the fridge and get some cheese, and then I get the cheese slicer from the drawer. I'm not allowed to use a sharp knife unless someone is with me, but maybe that rule isn't what I thought it was either? For a moment I think about this. And then I use the cheese slicer anyway because I don't want to cut my hand. Blood makes me feel sick.

I sit down to eat my sandwich and then I realise my right hand is still stinging really badly, and it seems to have mud on it too. But I don't care, and so I eat the sandwich anyway, muddy hands and everything.

Kaydee and Lissa come in while I'm at the kitchen table. They are giggling but they stop when they see me. Kaydee keeps smiling, but Lissa doesn't. 'All right, Darbs?' Kaydee says. She goes to the cupboard where the chocolate biscuits are kept.

'Yeah,' I say, because I am feeling a bit better since I started eating. And maybe now that Kaydee and Lissa are downstairs, they'll keep me company.

Kaydee says to Lissa, 'What do you want? We've got Kit Kats, Twirls and . . . er . . . Double Deckers.'

'Twirl,' says Lissa.

Kaydee takes one from the cupboard and gives it to her. Then she takes one for herself and they go out of the kitchen and I hear them running back upstairs.

'Can I come?' I shout, but they must not hear me because they don't answer, and I am alone in the kitchen again.

This day is turning out to be a really stinky one.

I remember . . .

. . . one day when Kaydee was off sick. Back then, she went to secondary school and I was still at primary. I begged and begged to be allowed to stay home with her. She had tonsillitis and was taking tablets from the doctor. Mum said no and no and no and no but I was so desperate to stay with Kaydee that I sat down on the stairs and wouldn't move. I was too big to be lifted into the car, though Dad did try. I gripped onto the banister and wouldn't let go, and even though they both shouted at me, I wouldn't budge.

In the end, Mum and Dad looked at each other, all tired, and I knew I'd won. I got a day off school and I spent all of it looking after Kaydee. I sat with her under a blanket on the sofa and we watched all four Spy Kids films, one after the other. And then we watched the Lion King films. Sometimes she would ask me to go and get her a drink or something to eat. And I did, because I felt proud and grown-up and responsible for her.

Mum popped in every now and then to see how we were, but Kaydee always said, 'It's all right, Mum. Darby's looking after me.'

Mum smiled and said, 'You're doing a great job, Darby,' and I felt happy.

At the end of the day, Kaydee said she was feeling much better and Mum said it must be because she had such an excellent nurse looking after her. I was very, very happy.

The next morning, Kaydee went back to school, so I did too. I was gutted because I wanted another perfect day like that.

Chapter 7

I watch some music videos in my room and practise the dance moves. I love nailing a routine. Sometimes they're too hard – lots of routines are really fast – but I just change bits to make them easier. I also find some cream in the bathroom cabinet that says it's good for stings, so I squeeze quite a lot of it out and rub it into my hand. And then I remember I haven't actually washed my hands, so I do that, and the cream washes off, but I put a load more on afterwards.

It's quite a while later when Mum calls up the stairs. I'm in the middle of a routine, so I don't do anything. And then she comes and knocks on my door and says, 'Come on, Darby, I've been calling you. Can you come and lay the table, please?'

'I'm busy,' I say, still trying to follow the video.

'You're *dancing*, Darby. You've done this one

twenty times already, I know. Come on, please.'

I sigh and switch off the laptop. Then I follow Mum down the stairs. The wind is still howling, and there's no sign of Dad or any of the other workers.

I lay the table, though I'm never sure if I've got the knife and the fork round the right way. My hand is still a bit sore but it's much better than it was and you can hardly see the white lumps. Mum is doing that thing she does when she's stressed: rushing from one side of the kitchen to the other, opening cupboards and dropping things or burning herself on the stove and pretend-swearing (you know, like 'sugar', which is what grown-ups say when they don't want to use rude words). Then she says, without even looking at the table, 'Right, Darby, can you call the others?'

I go to the bottom of the stairs and take a deep breath. I have a loud voice when I want to use it. 'DINNER!' I shout.

There's no response from upstairs but I wasn't expecting any. In our house, you have to say something at least three times before anyone takes any notice. So I shout, 'DINNER!' again, wait another ten seconds and shout it a third time.

Sure enough, I hear Olly shout back, 'All RIGHT!' and a thump of movement in his room. And I hear footsteps on the top flight of stairs up to Kaydee's room, so I know they're coming down too.

I can't take my eyes off Kaydee and Lissa when they come into the kitchen. They've done make-overs on each other, and they look *amazing*. Kaydee has shiny green eyeliner, like a sort of peacock colour, and it has tiny flecks of glitter in it. Her eyelashes have been curled and are thick with mascara, and her cheeks are faintly pink. Her lips are red and glossy. Lissa has the same kind of look but hers is even more dramatic, with purple eyeliner and dark plum-coloured lips.

'Wow,' says Mum, blinking slightly. 'You two look great.'

Olly glances at them, makes a sort of scoffing noise, and sits down.

'Is Paul coming in?' asks Kaydee. She's never got the hang of calling Paul 'Dad' because she remembers our first dad much more clearly than I do.

Mum shakes her head. 'Too much to do out there. So much to tie down and prepare. Anything to protect the plants, he's doing it.' She dishes up the food – beef stew with dumplings, one of my favourites – and hands round the bowls.

'Oh,' says Kaydee, suddenly looking horrified, 'I forgot to tell you, Mum. Lissa's vegetarian.'

There's a silence. Mum looks baffled. 'But we had sausages last time she came.'

'It's since then,' Lissa says. Her purple-streaked hair swings forward, brushing her smooth cheeks. 'I read a book about food production. It's disgusting the way animals are treated. And breeding cows for beef contributes to greenhouse gases and global warming. If we all stopped eating meat, we'd be a lot healthier, and so would the planet.'

I stare at her. Lissa, as far as I know, lives on Pringles and Dairy Milk. 'The planet isn't a person,' I say. 'It can't be healthy.' And I give a giggle to show how silly Lissa is.

'She means the planet needs certain things to keep supporting life,' Kaydee says gently. 'And the things that mankind does to it are damaging it.'

I blush and feel stupid.

Mum runs her fingers through her hair. 'I don't know what else we have.' She looks even more stressed. 'Do you eat fish, Lissa? I've got some tinned tuna.'

Lissa shakes her head. 'Sorry, no. Have you got any cheese?'

'Yes!' says Mum, relieved. 'Lots of cheese. Would you like to go and look in the fridge and see what you fancy? I'm sorry; I'd have made something else if I'd known.' She shoots a glance at Kaydee, who goes a bit pink.

'No worries,' says Lissa, skipping to the fridge. 'I'll have a cheese sandwich.'

'It's not exactly a hot meal . . .' says Mum, but Lissa isn't listening.

I eat an extra-big portion of my stew and enjoy every mouthful, though I notice that Kaydee only picks at hers. 'I'm thinking I might become vegetarian too,' she says.

'That's fine, Kaydee,' says Mum, in a voice that sounds like it's not quite as fine as all that, 'but we would need to discuss what you'd eat instead. You can't live on cheese sandwiches.'

There's a sudden gust outside and the window frame rattles, making us all jump. Lissa says a swear word (a proper one) and then laughs. I look at Mum. Her face is creased up with worry lines. 'It'll be OK, Mum,' I say, even though I have no way of knowing if this is true. And I lean over to

40

give her a hug, knocking over an empty glass by mistake.

'Be careful, Darby,' Mum says, standing it up again.

'Sorry,' I say. 'I was trying to hug you.'

She reaches over to hold my hand. 'Thanks, love.' Then she sighs and gives me a tight smile, one that presses her lips together and doesn't reach her eyes. 'We'll be all right. We've come through storms before.'

I remember . . .

. . . the last time. It was 20th February. It was really, really cold – so cold that I wore three pairs of socks when I was forced to go outside, and I had a pair of Hello Kitty hand warmers, the kind that heat up when you click the metal thing inside. The farm was smaller then, and Mum and Dad did *everything* themselves. Aunty Milly had to come and stay to look after me and Kaydee and Olly. She smelled of jasmine, which is a stinky smell, and she made me wash my hands all the time because she said I was picking my nose. I wasn't – I was covering my nose so I didn't have to smell her. But when I told her that, she told me off for being rude and she wouldn't let me have a sweet.

Mum and Dad were very stressed, and whenever I saw them they were too busy to talk to me. One time I clung to Mum's leg and she couldn't get out of the door, and she shouted at me and I burst into tears, and then she cried too, and then she hugged me, but she *still* went out to the farm instead of keeping me company. And Aunty Milly tried to hug me, but I threw up my dinner all down her back because of the jasmine smell.

Chapter 8

Pudding is treacle tart, my favourite. Lissa has seconds, with custard.

'What are you guys going to do after dinner?' Mum asks.

'I want to watch a film,' I say. I love film nights. We have a big sitting room with squishy sofas, and we all get comfy with cushions and blankets and settle in.

Kaydee looks at Lissa. 'What do you want to do?'

Lissa raises her eyebrows, and they both giggle.

'I'm busy,' Olly says curtly, which makes me jump because he's hardly spoken all mealtime.

I feel anxious. 'I want to watch a film.' It's suddenly important. And it's the only way I can think of to get Kaydee in the same room as me this evening. I've hardly seen her since Lissa arrived. 'Please.'

Olly looks at me. 'I'll only watch if it's something decent. *Not* Disney.'

I am disappointed. I love Disney.

'I'd watch *Captain America*,' Olly adds.

'Ugh, superhero films are so boring,' Lissa says. 'A load of men in tights prancing around saving the world. So sexist.'

'Did you know,' Kaydee says to us, 'that women in superhero films account for less than twenty per cent of speaking roles?'

'Darby can't watch *Captain America*,' Mum says. 'She'll get nightmares.'

This is probably true.

'Darby,' says Mum, 'why don't you go into the sitting room and pick three films you want to watch? Then everyone can vote.'

The light above the table suddenly flickers and we all look up. It stays on. The window rattles in another great gust of wind.

I go to the sitting room and look at the DVDs. Then I bring three of my favourites back to the kitchen.

After a lot of arguing, we decide on *Mamma Mia!* 'Go,' Mum says to us. 'I'll clear up.'

Kaydee and Lissa snuggle up under the big

blanket on one of the sofas. Olly goes to the other sofa and puts his feet up on the coffee table. He's brought his phone with him, and he'll probably just look at that all the way through the film.

'Have you got any popcorn?' Lissa asks.

'No,' Kaydee says, 'we hardly ever have popcorn. The last time we made it, Darby lifted the lid to see the corn, and it popped all over the kitchen floor.'

I remember . . .

. . . the popcorn. Kaydee said I could help her. We put a bit of oil in the bottom of the saucepan and tipped in the corn and turned up the heat. Kaydee put the lid on, and we waited to hear the popping noise. It takes a while to get going, but when it does, it sounds like there are fireworks going off inside. I really wanted to see the corn popping, so I lifted up the lid. Only I forgot to use the oven glove, and the knob of the lid was very hot, so I shrieked and dropped it on the floor, and it clanged loudly, and then all of a sudden the air was full of popcorn, bouncing out of the pan and landing on the floor. And Kaydee tried to pick up the lid but she burned her fingers too and then she got the giggles and so I got the giggles, and we were both scrabbling around on the floor while popcorn rained down on us. And the dogs rushed in and started trying to catch it, and that just made everything funnier.

Remembering this makes me laugh all over again. Lissa looks at me oddly, like I'm weird. Somehow that makes me laugh even more.

'Darby, are you going to laugh all the way through the film?' Kaydee asks, but she says it nicely.

I sit down next to Olly, still grinning. Lissa might have Kaydee for a bit, but she doesn't share the popcorn story!

Chapter 9

We're nearly at the end of the film. Bramble, our black Labrador, is lying on the sofa with his head on my knee. Pike stuck his whiskery face into the room earlier and walked over everyone on both sofas before deciding he'd rather be somewhere else. On the screen, Sophie is about to not get married, and Donna is singing a song about winners and losers.

Then the TV goes off. And so does the lamp. And there's a kind of *PTCHOOO* noise as all the electricity dies.

Three of us let out a wail. 'Oh, *what*?!' complains Kaydee. 'Not now!'

Olly jerks awake. 'What? Has it finished?'

'The power's gone off,' I tell him. As if to agree with me, the patio doors rattle really hard.

'Oh, for goodness' sake,' he says. 'This house is nuts.'

'It'll come back on again though,' Lissa says. 'I mean, we just have to wait a few minutes.'

'Yeah, right,' mutters Olly, throwing off the blanket and getting up. 'I'm gonna find a torch.' He bumps into the door on his way out and grunts in pain.

'Sometimes it can be off for hours,' Kaydee tells Lissa. 'Chances are, we won't get the end of the film tonight. Or any lights.'

'Seriously?' I can hear Lissa speaking, but I can't see her or Kaydee very well because it's dark. 'But it's only nine o'clock. What are we going to do now?'

There's a pause. 'We could listen to music in my room,' Kaydee says slowly.

'Can I come?' I ask. I don't like the dark. I don't mind it if there are other people around, but I don't like being on my own.

Somebody whispers something. Kaydee giggles, and then she says, 'Well, yeah, but it's OK if Darby comes, isn't it?'

Lissa gives a sigh, and then she says, 'We never get any time to ourselves though.'

I can feel my eyebrows jump up my forehead. 'You've had *all day* to yourselves!' I exclaim.

Kaydee says, 'You can come, Darby. It's OK.' She knows I don't like being alone in the dark.

Lissa says, 'Oh, all *right*.'

Mum comes to the doorway. 'You guys OK?' she asks. 'Sorry about this. To be expected. Just hope the energy board can get it up and running double-quick. I brought you some torches.'

'Thanks,' I say, taking one from her. Torches make shadows which are a bit scary, but it's better than being in the all-dark.

'It's bedtime really,' Mum says. 'Shall I come up with you, Darby?'

'We're going to Kaydee's room to listen to music,' I say.

Mum looks surprised. 'Oh. Right . . . Well, that's fine for half an hour, but then you need to get to bed, all right?'

'What about Kaydee and Lissa?' I ask.

'They should get to bed too,' Mum says, 'but they're older than you. They can make their own decisions.'

'I can make –'

'Darby, not now.'

'But I want –'

'Darby, I told you, you've got half an hour. Don't waste it arguing.'

I do a big huff, but I don't argue any more.

Kaydee, Lissa and I head up to Kaydee's bedroom, trailing blankets from the sitting room. I keep bumping into the walls and doorways as I go, because it's so hard to see, even with a torch. We have nightlights on the landing, but of course they're electrical, so everything is dark. As we reach the landing, Olly throws open his bedroom door, which makes me jump so much I nearly drop my torch. 'I'm out of juice,' Olly growls. 'Anyone got a portable charger thing for my phone?'

'I have,' says Kaydee. 'But I don't know where it is.'

'Can you look for it?' Olly asks.

Kaydee hesitates. 'I dunno where to start. I suppose it could be under my bed.'

'I'll look,' says Olly, starting up the stairs to Kaydee's room.

'No!' Kaydee races after him. 'There's all kinds of stuff under there! I'll do it.'

I follow the others up to Kaydee's room. Kaydee is half under her bed with Olly's torch. Only her bottom is sticking out. Her voice is muffled. 'If it's not here, then I don't know where it is . . . and I'm not spending all night looking . . . it's too dark to see properly.'

Lissa says, 'I like the dark. We use too much electricity anyway. It causes light pollution. That's why we can't see as many stars as we should.'

I really don't like Lissa. Everything she says is about how we're doing stuff wrong. 'Can we listen to music now?' I ask.

Olly doesn't hear me. He's staring at Kaydee – or what we can see of her. Which is mostly her bottom, in a skirt that's stretched all tight because she's wriggling on the floor. She looks very silly. I bend over and poke it.

'Ow! Darby, stop it.'

I laugh. 'It was Olly.'

'It was NOT!' says Olly furiously, much louder than I was expecting. His face is all strange in the torchlight. 'Forget it, all right?' He stomps down the stairs, hitting his head on the low bit of ceiling. '*Ow!*'

Kaydee wriggles out from under the bed. 'What was all that about? I can't find the charger. He'll have to live without his precious phone.'

'Can we listen to music now?' I say again.

'Yes, all right.' Kaydee still sounds annoyed. 'Honestly, brothers.'

'He's not even your *real* brother,' says Lissa as

we climb onto the bed. 'You're not related in any way.'

'He's been around long enough to *feel* real,' Kaydee says, and she rolls her eyes.

'Yeah,' I say, and I laugh. 'He's *such* a pain.'

Lissa cuts across me. 'What are we going to listen to?'

'I've got loads of music on my phone,' Kaydee says. 'Darby, you can choose first.'

'Can we have the strawberry song?' I say.

She smiles. 'Sure.'

'Which strawberry song?' Lissa asks.

'It's by The Beatles,' says Kaydee.

'The who?'

'The Beatles,' I repeat. They're the boy band that Dad likes. When he first told me their name, I thought they were called The Beetles, and for ages I wondered if they all had six legs and antennae. Then he wrote it down for me and I saw that it was spelled wrong. I guess the people in the band didn't know how to spell and it got stuck like that, and by the time anyone realised, it was too late to change it.

'Boy band back in the sixties,' Kaydee says to Lissa.

'Oh, *them*. That's ancient music.'

'It's still good,' I say, and then I stop talking because the song has started.

To my relief, Lissa doesn't talk through the song. She really seems to be listening. When the song plays, it makes me think of rows and rows of strawberry plants in the sunshine, with their ripe red berries all juicy and ready to be picked, just like we have every year here on the farm. There are no faces in jars in this song, which is a good thing. Instead, there are words that don't quite fit into the tune, which is how I feel sometimes. There's an extra-crazy bit just when you think the song has finished and I almost like it the best because it's saying, 'Go wild! Run around in strawberry fields!' – or that's how it sounds to me.

The three of us sit, warm under the blankets, with the torchlight making bat-shadows on the walls.

When the song finally dies away, there's a moment of silence. Kaydee has her arm around me, and her head is resting on top of Lissa's. It feels as though time has stopped, and a part of me wishes that this moment could last forever.

And then Lissa says, 'Is it my turn to choose now?'

Chapter 10

I wake in the night because of the noise. The wind is howling and the trees are whooshing and something outside is making a metallic dragging noise. Like a robot with an injured leg. Or a monster.

I lie under my duvet and listen, and I feel cold. I don't like the dark, and I don't like strange noises. I could reach out for the torch on my bedside table, but what if there is something in my bedroom too? What if, as I stretch out my hand, something grabs me? Or bites me? Or cuts my hand off completely?

I can't move. The metal scraping comes again, and again. And then a pause . . . and then again. *Scrape . . . scrape . . .*

I want Georgie. Georgie is a small giraffe I had as a baby. I took Georgie everywhere with me until I was seven and Mum persuaded me to leave her at home. Georgie is now under my bed, hidden away. Everyone else has forgotten about her, but I haven't. I like knowing she's there.

But I can't get out of bed and feel around in the dark. I'm too scared.

My eyes are wide open, staring at the ceiling. I can't cry. I can't move my head. This must be what it's like to be stone. You can't move, not at all. Maybe stones feel pain. Or fear. No one would know, because they can't tell you.

Scrape . . . scrape . . .

My mind fills with images of the metal monster outside, red and rusty, with yellow eyes that gleam menacingly in its battered head. It has bicycle spokes for ribs, and tin cans for hands, which reach out in the wind and scrape along the side of the house . . . *scrape . . . scrape . . .*

The scraping is closer now. It is outside my window. If I wait any longer, it will punch its steel fist through the glass. And then the monster will be *in my room . . .*

I leap out of bed, dragging my pillow with me, and run the five steps to my wardrobe. Pulling the door open, I squeeze inside, ducking under the hems of hanging dresses and tangling my foot in a thick woolly jumper. The pillow comes in too, squeezing into the small space between me and the door, which I pull closed behind me.

I sit very still, listening. But all I can hear is my own frightened breathing. Has the monster gone? Or is it peering in through my window with its glowing yellow eyes, trying to see through my thin curtains, wondering where I am?

Inside the wardrobe it is very dark, much darker than my room. But I can feel walls on all four sides of me, and I am holding the door shut so tightly that nothing and no one could open it. My fingers cramp but still I grip the door. I can't see anything. But I sit there, curled up, and wait for the terrifying growl that will tell me the monster has arrived.

Chapter 11

When the wardrobe door opens, I tumble out onto the floor, waking suddenly.

'Goodness, Darby!' Mum exclaims. 'Why are you in the wardrobe? Did you *sleep* in there?'

I rub my eyes, jolted from sleep to waking too quickly. My head feels fuzzy, and my neck is sore.

Mum is used to my not answering her questions. She helps me up from the floor and onto my bed.

I sit, moving my head from side to side.

She crouches in front of me. 'You OK? Sweetheart, you gave me such a fright. I come into the room and your bed's empty! Didn't you hear me calling?'

'No,' I say.

'In the *wardrobe*,' Mum says, like she can't quite believe it. 'Were you trying to get to Narnia again?'

'No,' I say. 'There was a metal monster.'

She raises her eyebrows. 'A metal monster? Where? In here?'

'Outside, trying to get in,' I say. 'I heard it scraping along the wall.'

She gets up and goes to my window, pulling open the curtain. 'Such a mess out there this morning,' she sighs. 'And the winds are getting up again. Oh – there. I think I've found your metal monster.'

I am nervous. Will it be out there, all twisted spokes and dented corners? Will the eyes still gleam or be dull and dead? My hands are shaking.

I look out of the window carefully. Mum points. 'Down there. Is that it?'

Right up against the side of the house, under my window, is a big metal oil can. As I watch, it slides a few centimetres sideways in the wind, scraping on the ground. The sound makes me shiver, even though I know it's not a monster after all.

Mum puts her arm around me. 'It's OK, Darby. No wonder you were scared. A noise like that, in the middle of the night, when the power's off and everything – well, I'd have been scared too.'

I turn into her arms and hug her back. I like

hugs. They make me feel safe, especially ones from Mum.

She kisses me on the head and says, 'The power's still off this morning, and something's wrong with the generator. Dad can't get it going. The ventilation and irrigation systems are all down.'

'Oh,' I say. This is bad. This is very bad, because the strawberry plants in the greenhouses need the right amount of water and other stuff. The plants are like babies. You can't just take away their air and food and expect them to be OK. I can tell Mum is very worried. So I say, 'Can I help?'

Mum makes a funny little noise, which sounds a bit like a sob. I didn't mean to make her cry! She squeezes me even tighter. 'Thanks, darling. You're such a good girl.'

It feels like there's a light inside me.

Mum takes a deep breath and steps back, looking into my face. 'You can't help on the farm. But you can help me at home. Can you be extra grown-up and look after yourself for most of the day? We have to get as much plastic off the tunnels as we can, so I've got to go out and help. The wind has died down a bit, but the forecast is for another storm, and we don't know how long the electricity will be off. I'll pop in to check up on you as much as I can. Will you be all right?'

I nod, seriously. 'Yup.'

She gives me another hug. 'Maybe you could play a board game with the others later. No one else is up yet – Olly's still snoring. I'll take my phone with me when I leave the house, so ring if there's an emergency.' She beams at me. 'You're brilliant, you are.'

I feel important and responsible. When Mum goes, I get back into bed for a bit. I am in charge of myself today. Soon I will get up and have breakfast, and then maybe do some dancing. My laptop will have some battery. Oh – if the electricity is off, the Wi-Fi will be off. I can't watch music videos.

Hmm. I don't really know what to do with my day. But my bed is very comfortable, and it's nice to stretch out after being in the wardrobe all night.

I wake up when there's noise outside my room – Kaydee and Lissa. I can hear them talking and laughing. I jump out of bed and throw open my door. Lissa is halfway up the stairs to Kaydee's room, clutching a bowl of cereal. Kaydee is on the landing behind her, also holding a bowl. They're both still in pyjamas. 'Hi,' I say.

Kaydee turns and smiles at me. 'Hi, Darby! You OK?'

'Yeah,' I say.

'Cool.' She turns and follows Lissa up the stairs.

I hesitate. I want to go up there too, but I haven't been invited.

Instead I go to the bathroom and do all the toilet and washing stuff. Well, a bit. Well, I run the tap. Washing is annoying. You have to get wet and I don't like the slippery feel of soap. Mum's always going on about germs, but I'm sure my hands are fine. I can't see anything dirty on them. I go back to my room and get dressed and go downstairs to the kitchen.

Pike, the black cat, is sitting on the kitchen table, licking his bottom. 'That's disgusting,' I say, and I lift him off. Then I decide what I would like for breakfast.

I sit alone at the kitchen table and look out of the window. I feel taller somehow. Older. When I've finished my cereal, I put my bowl and spoon in the dishwasher.

Now what?

I start thinking about chocolate. Tomorrow is the

chocolate hunt! And we will need the baskets. All four: red, green, yellow, blue.

The baskets are in Kaydee's room. I'll take them to the sitting room, ready for tomorrow morning.

I run up the stairs, excited.

I remember . . .

. . . the last chocolate hunt. Or maybe it was the one before. Kaydee, Dad, Olly and I were all waiting in the sitting room. Dad was messing around with Olly. Boys do that a lot, I've noticed. They were trying to give each other a dead arm. And then Olly did one on Kaydee, and she screamed and hit him with her basket and the handle came off. And then Dad hit Olly with his basket, and Olly hit Dad, and then Mum came in from the garden and said, 'Ready . . . go!' and Dad and Olly and Kaydee were so busy being silly with their baskets that they didn't even hear her. And Mum looked at me with twinkly eyes and said, 'Hurry up, Darby, you can get a head start.' And I ran out into the garden (but carefully because it was raining a bit) and started hunting. And that year I found ten more chocolates than anyone else, because the others were messing around.

And later, when we all came in again, Mum smiled at Dad and said, 'Well done,' and he winked at her, and I thought it was funny because he hadn't done well at all. If he hadn't been messing around with Olly and Kaydee, I wouldn't have got half as many as I did.

As I go up the stairs to Kaydee's room, I am thinking that I must check all the basket handles. And I don't bother knocking or anything; I just push open the door, and Kaydee and Lissa are on the bed together, and the cereal bowls are on the floor, and Kaydee and Lissa are . . .

. . . kissing.

I stand and stare, because they have their arms around each other and their eyes closed and that's all I have time to see before Lissa opens her eyes and notices me, and almost jumps off the bed in shock. 'What the . . .?' she says, with a really rude word at the end of it.

Kaydee sits up too. Her face is red, and she rubs her mouth and bursts out, 'DARBY!! What the hell do you think you're doing? Get out, get out!!'

And I am so frightened that I turn and run back down the stairs and into my bedroom and shut the door and curl up on my bed, shivering.

Chapter 12

A few minutes later, there is a knock at the door. The bed sinks slightly as someone sits on it. 'Darby,' says Kaydee quietly. 'Darby, I need to talk to you.'

I stay curled up in a ball. 'Go away.'

'Darby, please.'

'You shouted at me,' I say into my pillow. I like how the cotton feels. I rub my cheek against it.

'I'm sorry. I shouldn't have. I was . . . You took me by surprise. I didn't mean to upset you.'

I don't say anything. I wait.

'Darby, please sit up. I need to see your face.'

'Why?' I ask.

'Because I have to tell you something.' The bed moves a bit, and I know she's got up. I hear the bedroom door closing, and I think maybe she's gone out of the room, which seems kind of strange, so I uncurl and twist round to see. She's shut the door but she's still here. She comes to sit back down again, and her face looks really worried, and her eyes are all shiny.

'What?' I ask.

Kaydee waits for a moment and then she asks, 'What did you see, Darby?'

'You and Lissa *kissing*.' I make a puking face. Kissing like that, with your faces stuck together – well, it's kind of disgusting. I mean, it's all right in films of course. But seeing people in real life, right in front of me, doing it – it's embarrassing.

'Yeah . . .' Kaydee shuffles a bit on my bed. 'Yeah, we were.'

'You shouted at me,' I told her. That's what I mind. The kissing is embarrassing, but the shouting makes me feel bad. Kaydee never shouts at me – not like that. Not like she hates me.

'I'm sorry,' she says. 'I was . . . surprised. You . . . I didn't want you to see.'

'I didn't want to see either,' I tell her. 'It's disgusting.'

Her face goes red. 'It's not! Don't ever say that! Lissa and I . . . we love each other.'

'That's silly,' I say, a bit confused and not really sure what to say.

'Girls can love other girls.'

I know this. Of course I do. Girls can love girls, boys can love boys, a person can love girls *and* boys, Mum's told me that. That's not the point. I don't want Kaydee loving *anyone* more than she loves me. It scares me. What would I do if she didn't love me any more? Kaydee has always been the one looking out for me. Always – everywhere we go. I don't want her to be with Lissa. I want her to be with me, always. So I say, 'I'm telling Mum.'

Kaydee's face goes very angry. 'Don't you *dare*. This is *my* secret. *I* decide when I want Mum to know. *I* decide when to tell people. You keep your mouth shut.'

'Or *what*?' I say. I am angry now because she is angry and I'm afraid.

Kaydee looks at me, and her eyes are glaring, like they're going to shoot lasers at me. For a moment, I wonder if maybe she can actually do that and I'm going to be fried on the spot, my brain melted. 'Or I will take all your toys and throw them in the compost,' she says. 'And I will tear up all your paintings. And I will stamp on your earphones. And . . .' I brace myself for the horror she's saved till last. '. . . And I will get

Georgie out from the special secret place under your bed *and tear her apart.*'

I cannot speak. My eyes fill with tears.

Kaydee goes out of my room and shuts the door and I feel totally alone. Because Kaydee has often been angry around me – but she's never been angry *at* me before.

And I don't understand what I've done wrong.

I remember . . .

. . . a day at school. A boy called Rohan had started following me around. He called me Flat-Face and Slitty-Eyes and Big-Tongue, and lots of other unkind things. The teachers told him off, but he just waited until they weren't around and started doing it again. At lunchtime I was crying, and one of my friends went and told Kaydee what was happening.

Kaydee came swooping into my class in the middle of that afternoon's lesson. She ignored the teacher and stamped straight over to Rohan. 'Are you the one who's been bullying my sister?' she yelled.

Rohan didn't know who she was. 'What are you talking about?' he said.

Kaydee pointed at me. 'That's my sister, over there. Are you the one who's been making her cry?'

'I never touched her,' said Rohan.

The teacher tried to interrupt, but Kaydee just turned

round to her and said fiercely, 'My sister is being bullied because she has Down's syndrome, and this school is doing *nothing* to stop it. So *I'm* stopping it, right here, right now.'

The teacher just stared at her. I don't think she knew what to say. Kaydee faced Rohan again. She leaned forward and put her hands on his desk, so that he had to lean back out of the way. 'My sister is *beautiful*,' she hissed at him. 'My sister has the kindest heart of *anyone* I know. My sister is a better person than you will *ever* be. Having Down's syndrome doesn't make her weird or ugly or thick. It makes her *extraordinary*. Whereas you, small boy, *will only ever be ordinary.*'

Then she turned and went out of the room, nodding at the teacher as she did so. She hadn't come anywhere near me. But she didn't need to. Because I felt her support like an enormous cushion around me, protecting me, holding me up. Her fiery anger blew everyone over that day. Rohan never dared speak to me again. I think he was even afraid to say sorry. And the other kids in the class knew that if anyone, ever, said anything horrible to me, my big sister Kaydee would destroy them.

That's how it's always been.

Chapter 13

There's a knock at the door, and Olly comes in without waiting for a reply. 'Darby, have you got any spare batteries hidden in this cave of yours?' Then he stops. 'Darby. Hello? Are you OK?' He waves a hand in front of my face.

I can't speak. I really, really want a hug. Olly isn't a very huggy sort of person. But he is the only one here. So I reach out and put my arms around him and hold on very tight.

He says, 'Darby! Er . . . what are you doing? Um, this isn't . . . er . . . All right, all right.' I don't let go, so he has to sit down awkwardly next to me and put his arms around me too. It's not as good as hugging Mum because Olly has more angles. And he doesn't smell as nice. But it's still better than sitting on my own, hurting, and so I hold on for quite a long time.

'Is this about Kaydee and Lissa?' he says after a bit, in quite a gentle voice.

I am very surprised. I pull back. 'You know too!' I say. What a relief! Kaydee demanded that I didn't tell Mum, but if Olly already knows, then I'm not breaking any rules by talking about it with him. 'She shouted at me, Olly. Really shouted, and she said some horrible things.'

'Aww, I'm sorry.' He pats my arm. 'Did you get in the way?'

'No,' I say, annoyed. 'I wasn't anywhere near them. I only went up to get the baskets for the chocolate hunt. They didn't *have* to stop kissing.'

He goes very still. 'Wait . . . what? They were *kissing*?'

'Yes,' I say.

'Kaydee and Lissa,' he says.

I nod.

'Kaydee and Lissa . . . were kissing?' he says again.

'Yes,' I say, 'and I didn't mean to make her mad, but she says they love each other, and that means she doesn't love me any more, and I don't know what to do.' My lower lip starts to wobble.

But Olly doesn't put his arms around me again. Instead he stares at the wall. 'Kissing,' he says, in a voice that sounds kind of odd, like the inside of his mouth has been stung with nettles.

'What about me?' I ask, and big fat tears start rolling down my cheeks.

He stands up suddenly and kicks at the base of my bed. 'I *knew* it,' he says. 'I *knew* it.' Only there are rude words in between the other words. Then he turns his back on me and goes out of my room.

I am not sure whether I am less or more upset than I was before. This conversation has been confusing. I have a good think about it.

Mum asked me to be grown-up and responsible today.

Kaydee told me not to tell Mum about her and Lissa.

Olly is angry that Kaydee and Lissa were kissing. He's angrier about that than the fact that she shouted at me. Maybe he thinks girls shouldn't kiss other girls. Some people think it's wrong.

None of this thinking has helped me understand anything better.

I get some tissues and blow my nose and wipe my face. And then there's a kind of *pop* from somewhere downstairs, and the landing light comes on. There's a joyful shout from Kaydee's room, and I hear Olly say, 'Finally!'

That is a relief. If the electricity is on, I can play my music videos.

But I don't feel like dancing. I don't feel like anything really. I want to hide in bed and not talk to anyone or do anything.

Come on, Darby, I say to myself. You're not being grown-up and responsible about this. Who cares about stupid Kaydee and stupid Olly and even more stupid Lissa? Pull yourself together!

I grab my painting-by-numbers and my iPod and go downstairs to the kitchen table. I put on the overhead light, and the room feels warmer already. Then I sit down at the table, put in my earphones and start doing my painting. Pike jumps onto the table too and sits next to my paint pots. Bramble, in his basket, gets up and plods over to me. Then he lies down on my feet. He is quite a big dog and very warm. Soon my toes are toasty warm.

As I paint, I sing along to my music. I have lots of really good songs on my iPod, and I know all the words. Every now and then I put out a hand to stroke Pike. He has very soft black fur. He purrs and nudges my hand while I'm painting. Pike has no worries. All he wants is food and strokes. Bramble is the same. Animals have it easy.

I remember . . .

. . . when I was young I learned a song about animals at a fair. Which is weird because you don't get animals at a fair, you get them at a circus. Or sometimes not even there. Kaydee says circus animals are badly treated, which is sad.

The animals in the song were doing non-animal things. There was a baboon combing his hair, which isn't very likely because baboons don't have hairbrushes or hairdressers. They pick fleas out of their fur and eat them, which is totally disgusting. And in the song a monkey fell out of a bunk bed and nobody knows what happened to him. And an elephant sneezes, and I don't know if elephants can sneeze or not. They have very long noses, so maybe if they do sneeze, it's extra loud. I remember Kaydee asking Mum what had happened to the monkey, and Mum said with a smile that maybe the elephant fell on him and squashed him.

That poor monkey! I was so upset that I refused to sing the song ever again. And I haven't. I keep my promises.

Monica comes in, which takes me by surprise. She works on the farm. I like Monica: she has very black hair and eyebrows and she smiles a lot. I pause my music. 'Hi, Darby,' she says. 'Seen your mum?'

'Out on site,' I say.

Monica rolls her eyes. 'I keep missing her! She said she was coming back to the house, but she must have been held up.' She sighs. 'I need to sit. All right if I make a cup of tea?'

It's a bit like this in our house. People wander in and out and have cups of tea. I like Monica and I'd like some company, so I say, 'Yeah,' and she fills up the kettle.

'Thank goodness the electricity is back on, eh?' she says, nodding. When she's made her cup of tea, she sits down at the table. 'How are you today, Darby?' she asks.

I shrug. 'Fine.'

She laughs. 'You must be the only one. Everyone on the farm is in a . . . what's that? . . . right tizzy. A right tizzy.' She smiles. Monica isn't English but she loves collecting English sayings.

'Your hair is all tangled,' I say to her.

She reaches up to it. 'I know. Nightmare. It is the

wind. I should wear a hat. Or a bonnet. Or shave it all off, what do you think, eh?'

The thought of Monica with a shaved head makes me smile. 'You would look like an alien.'

'An alien!' She sits back in her chair and chuckles. 'Yes! Like ET!'

I remember . . .

. . . watching *ET*. It's a film about a short brown alien who comes to Earth and gets left behind by mistake. He meets a boy who makes friends with him and hides him in his closet (the American word for clothes cupboard, which is like a wardrobe but you wouldn't find Narnia at the back of it because the book's not called *The Lion, the Witch and the Closet*). I liked the bits with the children, but I found ET really gross. He's all wrinkly and poo-coloured and talks funny. And his finger lights up, like it's got a torch inside it. I wouldn't want him in my closet.

Monica would look nothing like ET. I was thinking of the other kinds of aliens, the ones that have smooth grey skin and long thin bodies and huge black eyes. Olly has a poster of them on his wall. But explaining all of that to her seems like too much of an effort, so instead I just nod and say, 'Yeah.'

'Can I see your painting?' she asks, leaning forward.

I turn it round so that it's facing her. It's a picture of a circus, with a big top and clowns and an elephant and some excited people in the audience, and children laughing.

Monica smiles. 'That's beautiful, Darby. You are very clever.'

'I just put the paint where it tells me to,' I say. 'It's simple.'

'You would be surprised,' she says, 'how often people don't understand something simple. Just follow an instruction.' She sighs, and the smile fades away.

I look at her. Monica has been smiling and laughing, but I think maybe she's only pretending to be happy. I reach over the table and put my hand on top of hers. 'You look sad,' I say.

She glances at me, surprised. Then she takes my

hand and squeezes it. 'You are clever in lots of ways, Darby. I *am* sad. I am sad when your parents are worried. They are good people. They look after their workers. And they do not deserve this.'

I nod, wondering what she means by 'this'. Does she mean the storm?

Monica holds my hand with both of hers. It is like my hand is in a cosy nest. Bramble is still on my feet. I am warm all over. 'Sometimes it is hard to know what God has in mind for us.'

Monica is a big believer in God. She prays every morning and every evening, and sometimes at other times too. She believes that God controls the weather. Dad doesn't think this because he doesn't believe in God. But then he says he checks the Met Office updates 'religiously', which is a bit odd. I don't know what I think.

I stop listening to Monica because I'm thinking about Met Office satellites and whether they bump into God up there above the Earth. But it doesn't matter because Monica has bowed her head and is mouthing some words. I'm pretty sure she's praying. When she's finished, she lifts her head and smiles at me, and then she says, 'It's a great comfort to know someone is listening.'

I am not sure if she is talking about me or God – and if she is talking about me then she is wrong, because I wasn't listening.

I want to tell Monica about Kaydee. But she gets up, letting go of my hand, and says, 'I'd better get back to work. Tell your mum I'll see her later.' She drinks the last of her tea and smiles again. 'After the storm comes the sun, eh, Darby?'

I smile back, but she's not right because the sun doesn't always come out after a storm. Sometimes all you're left with is a big mess that needs clearing up, and it's *still* grey and miserable.

Chapter 14

By the time Mum comes in I have finished three pictures, even though Pike kept distracting me by nudging my hand. One of the pictures has a cat paw print on it, which is a bit of a shame. Bramble got up when I had to go to the loo and he went back to his basket, so my feet are cold again. Marmite, our other dog, is always out on the farm. He's a springer spaniel, and he's got more energy than Bramble. If he sat on me, it would only be for about two seconds.

'Darby!' says Mum, coming over and giving me a hug. 'How are you, love? Oh, look at your beautiful paintings! You clever thing.'

'Pike tried to help,' I say, showing her the paw print.

Mum laughs. 'As long as it was his paw and not his bum.'

'He was cleaning his bottom on the table again,' I say.

Mum screws up her nose. 'And people say cats are such good pets. How revolting. I'll spray the table. Make sure you wash your hands. It's kind of chilly, don't you think?'

'My feet are cold,' I tell her.

'Why don't you nip upstairs and get yourself an extra pair of socks? I'll put the heating on. In the meantime, I'm going to make some soup. Can you tell Olly and the girls that lunch will be in five minutes?'

The girls. That's what she usually calls me and Kaydee. Now it's Kaydee and Lissa, and where does that leave me?

I go up and knock on Olly's door. 'What?' he grunts.

'Lunch in five,' I say through the door.

He grunts again. I'm not sure if that means he's coming down or not.

I don't want to go up to Kaydee's room because I am afraid she will shout at me again. So I call up the stairs, 'Lunch in five!' and then go to my room before they can reply.

I pull on my biggest and warmest jumper, and I

put on another pair of socks. Our house is usually quite warm, but when there's a storm the wind seems to find all the little gaps in the door and window frames. I hear the *clunk* of the heating as Mum switches it on.

I lay the table for Mum and put cheese and bread and butter out too. She chatters at me. 'There's not too much damage after all that noise last night. The wind caught one of the polytunnels and bent the frame. Your dad's working as fast as he can to get the plastic off the rest of the tunnels. Juris has called in all his mates to help. There's another storm forecast for tonight. Can you believe this weather? Thank goodness the electricity is back on. They're good, the engineers, but they have to prioritise. Old people's homes are more important than our fruit. Though if we lose the crops . . . Well, let's hope that doesn't happen. Too many people depend on us. Have to keep fighting, don't we? We'll muddle through some-how . . . Monica told me she'd popped in to see you earlier.'

I nod.

'She's a diamond, that woman,' Mum goes on. 'I hope she can stay. She's got family problems back home. She's one in a million; we'd never find anyone like her if she and Gregor had to go.'

Mum sometimes forgets that I don't follow fast talking very easily. She keeps going, but I got lost somewhere between 'polytunnels' and 'fruit'. I sit down at the table and wait.

There are footsteps on the stairs, and Kaydee and Lissa come in. I don't want to look at them. I am afraid that Kaydee is still angry with me. They are laughing and chatting and asking if the electricity will stay on. 'I don't know,' Mum says in reply. 'How long is a piece of string?'

This is a weird thing grown-ups say when you ask them a question they can't answer. I don't know what string has to do with anything. Maybe it's because string can get tangled and so can conversations.

I remember . . .

. . . playing with string in the garden with Pike. I dangled it in front of his nose and he batted it with his paws. It made me laugh, and I waved it around in the air, and Pike tried to catch the end of the string as it went past him, and I bent down to tease him, and he swiped at the string with his paw, and he scratched me right across one cheek. It stung a lot and I had two red scratches on my face when I went to school the next day. I told people the cat had scratched me and they all looked shocked. And the teacher was extra nice to me because I had a hurt face, and Leila let me borrow her nicest pen.

Kaydee sits down next to me, which makes me nervous. Is she going to shout again, or is she going to pretend that nothing happened? She doesn't look at me, but she does say, 'Hey, Darby,' and then carries on talking to Mum. I think she is going to pretend everything is fine, which means I have to pretend too. I am not very good at pretending.

Olly comes in and he is even worse at pretending than I am. I can see by his face when he looks at Kaydee that he is still furious. His eyes are red too, like he's been crying. Maybe he feels as sad as I do that Kaydee loves Lissa. He sits down next to me, and I reach to hold his hand, because I want to let him know that I understand – but he snatches it away and says, 'Pass the butter.'

It is a funny meal. It's like the Magic Eye picture that Dad put up on the landing. It looks like squiggles, but if you look at it long enough, you're meant to see a picture beneath the squiggles. I can't do it – my eyes don't work like that – but this meal is like those pictures. Like we are a lot of squiggles but there's a hidden picture underneath. We are a kaleidoscope of people, sitting and talking to each other, the conversation shifting and changing into different patterns, and everyone is not-quite looking at each other, not-quite laughing properly.

It is a table of not-quite people. All squiggly.

I can't see the pattern underneath but I know it's there.

Chapter 15

I think if Mum weren't so worried about the farm, she might have noticed something's wrong with all of us. But her eyes keep sliding to the windows, and she tries to butter her cheese instead of her bread, so I don't think she's really paying attention.

'Darby,' says Olly unexpectedly, 'want to play a game after?'

I blink. 'After what?'

'After lunch,' he says, like I'm an idiot.

'Oh.' I can't remember the last time Olly asked me if I wanted to play a game. I am a bit confused. 'What game?'

He shrugs. 'I dunno.'

'That's a nice idea,' Mum says. 'Maybe all four of you could play together.'

There is a stung silence, like the split second after someone has smashed a glass on the floor.

'It's a two-player game,' says Olly.

'You just said you didn't know what you were going to play,' Kaydee says.

'You've got your own two-player game going on,' Olly says, and his voice sounds hard and cold, like ice.

Mum doesn't notice that they're glaring at each other. She is clearing away the bowls and looking out of the window again.

Kaydee turns to me. 'Thanks for *nothing*, Darby.' Then she gets up and leaves the room. Lissa goes after her.

I burst into tears. Olly puts his arm around me. 'Sorry, Darbs,' he says.

Mum says, 'Oh gosh, Darby, what's the matter?' She fetches the tissue box and comes to sit the other side of me.

I can't tell her. It's a secret. I wasn't supposed to tell Olly, I see that. I made a mistake. Now Kaydee thinks I can't be trusted. I have to prove that I can still keep secrets, which means I can't tell Mum. Not now, not ever.

'It's not your fault,' Olly says.

'What's not her fault?' asks Mum, passing me another tissue.

Olly hesitates and looks at me. He mustn't tell! 'Kaydee and Lissa,' he says slowly, 'are best friends. Darby feels left out.'

'Oh, sweetheart!' Mum reaches out to hug me. 'Darling, we've talked about this. Kaydee will *always* be your sister. She will *always* love you. But she is allowed to have other people in her life. People her own age, who have the same interests as her.'

Olly makes a kind of snorting noise, and then he coughs straight after to make it sound like an accident.

'You and Kaydee can spend all of Monday together when Lissa goes,' Mum says. 'Why don't I drop you in town next week and you can go bowling, just the two of you?'

I *love* bowling. I nod quite hard.

'There.' Mum kisses me on the head. 'Oh dear, I don't want to leave you if you're in a state. But I really ought to go out again.'

'I'll look after Darby,' Olly says, and I nearly fall off my chair in surprise.

'I thought you were joking,' I say.

He looks offended. 'I'm not joking. You can play Spooky Manor with me if you like.'

96

Spooky Manor is a game we can play on the TV using the controllers. It's brilliant, all about finding jewels in a haunted house. I smile at him. 'Cool!'

There's another *PTCHOO!* and the lights go out again.

Mum lets out a very, very big sigh. 'Oh no, I don't believe it. That's just typical.'

'There goes Spooky Manor,' I say. I should have known. This is a Bad Day. This is not one of those days where Nice Things Surprise You.

'Sorry, Darbs,' says Olly. 'Er . . . what do you want to do instead?'

Mum reaches over and ruffles Olly's hair, which I know he hates. 'You are a good boy,' she says. 'I've got to go out. Your dad will be doing his nut over this. I bet the vents are jammed open now – that'll be disastrous if the wind picks up again.' She gets up, shaking her head. 'Sometimes I think we must be mad to do this . . .'

I have an idea. 'I want to build a den,' I say.

I remember . . .

. . . when Kaydee and I were much, much younger, we used to build dens all the time. Sometimes in the garden, but mostly indoors. The house was smaller then, before Dad built the extension. The sitting room was the same size though, and Kaydee and I used to bring all the spare sheets down and drape them over the chairs and anything we could find to make a kind of tent. Then we would crawl underneath with torches and packets of crisps and tell each other stories and sing songs.

And very, very occasionally, Mum would let us sleep in the den, all the way through the night. And those were the best nights ever.

Chapter 16

Olly is actually better than Kaydee at building a den because last year he did an engineering course and so he knows about structure and bridges and things. At least, this is what he says. He even has this idea about suspending sheets from the ceiling, using a rope and pulley system. He says it will be amazing.

But it's slower than building a den with Kaydee, to be honest, and I get a bit impatient because it's taking so long. 'Hurry up,' I say.

Olly is really into it. 'Can you get me the clothes pegs, Darby? And some string.'

I sigh. 'Oll*eeeee*.'

'Go on. This is going to be the best den ever, I promise.'

I go and get the pegs and the string. 'Cool!' says Olly. 'Stand here, and hold this . . .'

I stare out of the window as I hold one corner of a sheet. Outside, the sky is full of chasing clouds, bumping into each other. I bet clouds don't like storms. Storms are loud and pushy and shoot lightning. I bet clouds get scared. No wonder they're all running away.

'Darby!' Olly interrupts my thoughts. 'Don't do that talking-to-yourself thing. It's weird.'

I sigh again.

And then Olly says, 'All right, you can let go . . . ta-da!'

And he pulls on the string, and the sheet canopy lifts up off the ground like a big white parachute, leaving just enough space to crawl under. '*Whoa!*' I say. And then I dive underneath, yelping and whooping, and Olly does the same, and it's like we're little kids again, shouting while we play, 'Pirates boarding the starboard side!' and, 'Pass the space blaster!' Olly pretends he's firing a huge gun, with a really good explosion noise, and I fight off the pirates with a sword (well, a bent dog chew) and we put one of those torches that stands up by itself underneath and make shadow shapes with our hands on the sheets. Both of us get louder and louder until Olly stands up suddenly and says, 'I know where

Doctor Death is!' and hits his head on the mantel-piece and collapses, swearing.

I crawl over to him and say, 'Don't worry, I'll deal with Doctor Death!' and Olly says crossly, 'Leave it, Darby, I'm not playing any more.'

I sit quietly while he rubs his head. 'Can we play again when you feel better?' I ask.

'No.' He scowls. 'What a day.'

I don't know what to say to this, so I don't say anything. It's one of those phrases where you're not sure if the other person needs an answer.

Olly sits up, still with his hand clutched to his head. 'Why are girls so weird, Darby?' he groans.

'I'm not weird,' I say.

He gives me a sort of grin. 'I didn't mean you. You're not weird. Dappy, but not weird.'

I grin back at him. Dappy is fine. Dappy means a bit away-with-the-fairies, like you're not really paying attention. And that's definitely what I am.

'You never know what they're thinking,' Olly complains. 'Girls. They spend so much time on hair and make-up when they look fine without it. But they don't like it if you tell them that. And they do all this whispering and giggling and inviting you to join in, and then they get annoyed when

101

you say the wrong thing. Why don't they just *tell* you what you're supposed to say?'

I shrug. 'I dunno.'

'I never get it right,' Olly says, shaking his head. 'If there's a girl I like, she never likes me back.'

He sounds bitter, and his mouth is all screwed up like he's just tasted a lemon.

'But *they* won't ask you out if they like you, oh no. You're supposed to *guess*. And get laughed at if you're wrong. It's like some massive game where no one tells you the rules.'

I look at him, surprised, because this is how I see the whole world really. As a big game with confusing rules. 'You should make your own rules,' I say.

Olly gives a sort of laugh. 'I wish,' he says. 'That's not how it works. Maybe I should become a hermit.'

I laugh. 'You can't be a hermit. You're a human.'

He rolls his eyes. 'Do you even know what a hermit is?'

'Yeah,' I say, though I'm not actually sure.

'A hermit,' says Olly, 'is someone who lives on his own. Outside society.'

'Oh,' I say. That isn't what I thought it was. 'I don't want to live on my own.'

'You don't have to, Darby,' Olly says. 'You'll probably never live on your own.'

I smile. 'Good. I don't want to be lonely. And I don't want you to be lonely, Olly. You can come and live with me.'

He smiles now. 'Thanks, Darby. Never turn into one of those girls, OK? The ones who laugh in your face.'

'I promise,' I say.

Neither of us says anything for a bit. I start thinking about chocolate, which is what often happens. 'I can't wait till it's the chocolate hunt,' I say.

'You and your chocolate hunt,' he says.

'I like the pink ones best.'

'Darby, under the foil, it's all the same chocolate.'

'No, it isn't,' I say.

'It is!'

'It isn't!'

He stares at me, shaking his head. 'I bet if they were all unwrapped, you couldn't tell which was which just by eating them.'

'I could,' I say indignantly.

'You *so* couldn't.'

'I so could!'

'Fine.' Olly crawls to the edge of the den. 'I'm going to test you.'

'What?' But he's gone. I wait. What does he mean, he's going to test me?

Olly is back within a minute, holding a packet I recognise very well. I gasp. 'You can't take that! It's for the hunt!'

'Oh, come on,' Olly says. 'Mum's got loads of them. She won't notice if one's missing.'

'We shouldn't take it. I'm not supposed to take snacks without asking.'

'You didn't take it. I did,' Olly points out.

'But . . .'

He opens the packet, and a deliciously tempting scent of chocolate wafts over to me. I *loooove* chocolate. *So* much.

Olly says to me, 'Close your eyes. We have to do this scientifically.' He sounds like a teacher.

I close my eyes. I hear him unwrapping the chocolates, and I breathe in the lovely smell.

'Right,' says Olly, 'keep your eyes closed. No cheating. Give me your hand.' He puts a round chocolate in my hand. 'Put it in your mouth before it melts.'

I do so. The chocolate slides across my tongue. Mmmm.

'What colour was the wrapper?' he asks.

I open my eyes and smile at him. 'Pink.'

Olly's eyes narrow as he looks back at me in the torchlight. 'Yes . . .' he says. 'Hmm. Right, next one.'

I close my eyes and hold out my hand. Another chocolate. Yum. 'Blue,' I say.

'You're cheating,' says Olly.

'I'm not!' I say.

'Then you're just making lucky guesses,' he says. 'Close your eyes again.' This time he shuffles around so that he's unwrapping the chocolate away from me.

'Yum,' I say, biting down through the softness. 'Pink again.'

'Ha!' Olly says, triumphant. 'Wrong! That one was gold!' He shows me the wrapper.

'I meant gold!' I say. 'Try me again.'

By the time the packet is empty, I have guessed right more times than wrong.

'How are you doing it?' Olly asks.

'I told you, they taste different,' I say, though I am feeling a bit weird in my tummy now. I think maybe I shouldn't have eaten the whole lot.

He looks impressed. 'I didn't think you could do it.'

I grin. I love it when people say that.

I remember . . .

. . . a long time ago, Mum took me to a talk at the museum. It was by a man who knew lots and lots of stuff about beetles and other insects. He showed us photos of enormous butterflies and tiny ants. And he had brought along some real, live insects too, that we could hold after the talk. I held a stick insect, and a stag beetle. And then I reached out for the big, furry tarantula.

The beetle man looked at me and put his head on one side. He said, 'Are you sure? This spider is very friendly, but she doesn't like sharp movements. If you jerk your hands, she'll be frightened. And then she might bite you. You have to keep your hands very still.'

Mum said, 'Darby, you don't have to hold the spider.' She was pale and wobbly.

I said, 'I want to,' and I held out my hands.

Carefully, the beetle man put the tarantula into my

hands, and I stayed very calm. The beetle man nodded, and then he started telling me all about tarantulas and how they're not as scary as people think, and how it's like holding a big hamster really.

I could hear whispers. Some of the other children looked frightened. But I thought the spider was interesting, not scary. It was kind of tickly actually.

When I gave the spider back, the beetle man asked if anyone else would like a turn. And everyone else said no thank you. I was the *only one* brave enough.

On the way home, Mum said to me, 'I can't believe you did that, Darby. I'd never have guessed you would.'

I like surprising people.

Chapter 17

I was cheating in the chocolate game, of course. I opened my eyes just a tiny bit to see the colour of the foil. Sometimes I couldn't see clearly; sometimes my eyes weren't quite sure of the colour, since the light wasn't good. But I was definitely cheating.

I'm not telling Olly though.

We pull all the cushions off the sofas and put them on the floor under the canopy and lie down on them. I am feeling a bit sick from all the chocolates, and also sleepy. Sleeping in wardrobes is not very good for you. And Olly can doze anywhere, since he stays up so late playing video games. So it's not long before we are both asleep.

That's where Mum finds us later. She smiles at me, but her face is all creased, like a screwed-up piece of paper. 'Hi, Darby,' she says gently.

I am warm and sleepy and fuzzy. 'Hi, Mum.' I give her a hug.

'Thanks, sweetheart.'

Olly is snoring next to me. Mum beckons me out from under the sheets. 'Guess what?' she whispers. 'I thought we might order pizza for tea. What do you think?'

I think, I *love* pizza. Not as much as chocolate, but it's close.

Mum and I order pizza on the old-fashioned phone, the one that only needs a phone line, not electricity. We order Four Cheese, Meat Feast, Spicy Chicken, and Vegetable (for Lissa). Mum adds on a couple more for Juris and Monica because they've all been working flat out today and haven't had time to eat properly. And then we add garlic bread and Diet Coke. Mum looks a bit pale when she hears the total cost, but she reads out her credit-card number anyway.

When the pizzas arrive, Kaydee and Lissa come downstairs. They've done another makeover on each other, with hairstyles too. Olly sees them and sighs. I remember what he said earlier about girls looking fine without make-up, but I think they both look amazing.

'Wow,' says Mum. 'You two are so good at this. Can you do Darby too?'

I feel like a light switches on inside me. 'Oh, YES,' I say. 'Yes, do me, do me!'

So after dinner, Kaydee brings down her hair stuff and her make-up kit (which is *huge*) and Lissa's make-up kit (which is even *huger*) and she sits me on the kitchen chair, and she and Lissa look at my face in a considering way. Then they get started.

First they wipe stuff all over my face with a cotton-wool ball, and then they wipe other stuff all over it. And then the foundation goes on. Then I have to close my eyes while they apply eyeshadow. Then they do powder, and some of it goes up my nose and makes me sneeze. Then there's eyeliner, and mascara, and blusher, and lip liner and lip tint.

And all the time they are talking.

'My mum taught me how to do make-up when I was nine,' Lissa says.

'Really?' Kaydee sounds impressed. 'Wow. My mum doesn't know one end of a mascara from the other.'

'Mum said it was important to know how to do it properly,' Lissa says. 'She wears it all the time. That *man* used to have a go at her about it.'

'He was no good for her,' Kaydee says, screwing the top back on the foundation. 'She's better off without him. So are you.'

'Yeah,' Lissa says. 'Totally.'

Kaydee says, 'She should have chucked him out years ago. Not waited for the police to get him.'

I have not really been listening, but now I am. 'The police?' I say.

Kaydee glances at Lissa. 'My dad's in prison,' says Lissa.

I am completely shocked. 'Prison?' I say. 'Why?'

'Drugs,' says Lissa.

'Oh,' I say. 'Drugs.' I don't know much about drugs, except they are bad.

'He was dealing,' Lissa continues. 'He was bound to get caught in the end. Mum kept telling him to stop. He kept promising to go straight and get a proper job. But then he'd go back to dealing.'

I'm a bit lost again. 'Dealing' is what you do with cards, like when you play Snap. I don't think this can be the same kind of dealing.

'Do you miss him?' Kaydee asks.

Lissa shrugs. 'Not really. I used to go and visit him. But it was horrible. Really scary. So I kicked off and said I wouldn't go any more. Mum doesn't go either now. Says he's a waste of space.'

So Lissa doesn't have a dad. Or not a good one anyway. 'You should get a stepdad,' I tell her. 'Like we have.'

She laughs, and for a moment I am surprised because I don't think I've actually heard her laugh before. It's quite a nice sound. 'Yeah, right,' she says. 'Cos it's that easy.'

'Your mum should go on the Internet,' I say. 'On a dating site.'

'Darby!' Kaydee sounds scandalised. 'How do you know about dating sites?'

How old does she think I am? '*Everyone* knows about dating sites,' I say.

Kaydee and Lissa look at each other and laugh. 'What's a dating site, Darby?' Kaydee asks me.

I know she knows what one is. She's trying to trick me. 'Aha,' I say, wagging my finger at her. 'You can't catch me out that way.'

Lissa laughs again. 'Would you go on a dating site one day?' she asks me.

'No way!' I say. 'They're full of creeps and strangers.'

For some reason this makes them both laugh even more.

'Mum says a stranger is just a friend you haven't met yet,' Kaydee reminds me, grinning.

'Mum,' I say, putting my hands on my hips, 'is a very trusting person.'

Lissa is laughing so hard that tears are coming out of her eyes and making black smudgy marks at the corners. 'Your sister is so funny,' she gasps to Kaydee.

I feel about ten centimetres taller. Maybe Lissa isn't so bad after all.

Chapter 18

They do my hair after they've done my face, putting little plaits at the sides and pinning them back. 'You look really cute,' Lissa tells me.

Kaydee says, 'I'm going to get a mirror,' and runs out of the room.

There's a bang from across the hall, and Dad comes clomping into the house in his work boots. 'Dad!' I call. I haven't seen him since yesterday morning; he's been so busy with the storm damage and trying to look after the farm.

He comes to the kitchen doorway and sees me sitting on the chair, and his eyebrows move right up his forehead like they're trying to climb into his hair. 'Darby?!' he says, as though he's not sure it's me.

I get off my chair and stand in front of it, one hand on my hip, like a model. I toss my head so that my hair swishes. 'What do you think?' And then I do a sort of twirl.

'Well . . .' says Dad. The lines across his forehead vanish completely and the corners of his blue eyes crinkle instead as he smiles at me. He rubs his nose with a grubby finger. 'Well . . . I think you look like a princess.'

I beam at him. Behind him, Kaydee says, ''Scuse me! Mirror coming through!'

I have to look very hard at my reflection because it doesn't look anything like me. My eyes are lined in dark brown and covered in the same kind of glittery eyeshadow that Lissa and Kaydee were wearing yesterday. My eyelashes look a lot longer and darker than usual, and Kaydee used some kind of clamp thing to make them curl upwards. Even though I've had to put my glasses back on, you can still see the effect.

I look beautiful.

I want to look like this every day.

'You like it?' Kaydee asks, smiling.

'I *love* it,' I say. 'Thank you.'

Kaydee and Lissa nod at each other.

'Good work, girls,' says Dad. He heads to the cupboard in the corner of the room and rummages around. He pulls out a small plastic thing and pops out two tablets. Dad gets stress headaches. It's not very surprising that he has one today.

'Lissa,' says Kaydee, 'you should draw Darby.'

Draw me? What does she mean?

'Lissa does the most amazing portraits,' Kaydee explains.

Lissa looks embarrassed. 'Oh, stop it.'

'I'm serious! Draw her. Go on. She'd love it. I'll get you some paper.'

Lissa hesitates. I like the idea of someone drawing a picture of me, especially looking like this. 'Please,' I say.

She gives a shrug. 'All right. But don't expect . . . I mean, I'll do the best I can.'

I nod. Of course. To be honest, anything she can draw will be about a billion times better than anything I could draw. Drawing is not something I can do.

I remember . . .

. . . coming home from school with a painting I'd done. I was really proud of it. It was a rainbow over meadows, and I'd done some sheep in the fields too. 'Darby, that's wonderful,' Mum said, giving me a hug. 'I love it. We'll put it up on the fridge.'

And then Kaydee came in from her school, holding a plastic art folder, and she said, 'They let me bring this home now it's been marked.' And she took it out . . . and it was this amazing, detailed pattern in black, white and blue, filling the whole page. It must have taken hours and hours.

Mum was speechless for a moment. And then she said, 'Kaydee, that's absolutely brilliant. Goodness, you clever thing.'

And all the happiness that had filled me up like a balloon came kind of leaking out. Because it was so, so much better than mine, and even though Kaydee is four years older, I knew that I would never, ever be able to do anything as good as that.

So later, when no one else was around, I went and took down my picture, tore it up and hid it at the bottom of the bin. And when Mum asked me if I knew what had happened to it, I pretended I didn't.

Kaydee fetches Lissa a pencil and rubber and a large piece of paper, and she starts to draw me. I hear Mum and Dad talking quietly in the hallway and I really want to call out to Mum. I want her to see how I look. But Lissa is concentrating, so I know I should wait until she's finished.

I am quite good at sitting still. A song by The Beatles starts playing through my head. It's about a girl called Lucy and she's got diamonds in the sky. I like the words in the song because they make pictures in my mind. They sing about tangerine trees, and that makes me think of orange trees (not trees with oranges on but trees that are actually orange) and rivers of peanut butter, and grass made of liquorice. And I wonder what the girl called Lucy looks like. Maybe she looks a bit like me, now that I am all made up and beautiful. I would like diamonds. I would like a necklace of diamonds, and a bracelet and earrings to match. And a hair clip of diamonds too.

'Darby, stop moving,' Kaydee says, and I blink.

'I wasn't,' I say.

'Yes, you were. Stop looking up at the ceiling and talking to yourself.'

I frown.

Lissa says, 'Don't worry, you're fine.'

'See?' I stick out my tongue at Kaydee.

Lissa laughs. 'Don't do that though. Princesses definitely don't stick their tongues out.'

She looks totally different this evening, and I don't mean because of the makeover. It's like all the spiky parts have been rubbed away. She looks softer, gentler, friendlier.

Lissa looks happy.

I still don't want Kaydee to love her more than me, but if Lissa is going to be nice to me, and do my hair and make-up and draw pictures of me, then I don't mind her being around.

Maybe Lissa and Kaydee could get married and I could be their bridesmaid. I would love a long pink dress, with diamantés round the neckline. They're like diamonds only not as expensive. And I would hold a bunch of white roses.

'Darby, you're doing it again,' Kaydee says.

'What?'

Lissa laughs. 'It's all right. I've just about finished anyway.'

Kaydee leans over to see the paper. 'Oh wow, Lissa. That's brilliant.'

'I want to see.' I'm not sure if I'm allowed to get

off my chair, but Lissa brings the drawing to me.

'There you go.'

I stare at the picture. Sitting on a chair, with a round face and serious expression, is me – but extra, extra beautiful. 'Wow,' I say. 'Wow. I look beautiful.'

'You are beautiful,' Lissa tells me. Then her expression changes, as if she's surprised, and she turns away to the kitchen table.

'I have to show Mum,' I say, and I get up and go into the hallway. Mum and Dad aren't there any more, so I turn left for Mum's study. The door is open a bit, and I can see Mum sitting at her desk, so I go in. 'Look at this! And look at me!'

Then I realise she's crying. She looks up, startled, her eyes wet. 'Oh!' she says, wiping them quickly. 'Darby, sweetheart.' She reaches out to put an arm around my waist. 'Goodness, don't you look grown-up! You OK?'

'Yes,' I say. I show her the drawing.

She takes it from me, smiling at it. 'Beautiful. Did Kaydee draw this?'

'No, Lissa,' I say.

'She's very talented,' Mum says. She smiles again. 'She's captured you perfectly. What a lovely portrait. Did you say thank you?'

'Yes,' I say, and then I frown, because actually I don't think I did. 'No.'

'We must frame it,' Mum says. Then she sighs and says, 'You should get to bed soon, darling. It's getting late.'

I put my arms around her because I can tell she's still sad, even though she liked the drawing. She hugs me back. 'Oh, Darby,' she says, 'you do give the best hugs.'

I am good at hugs, I know.

'Don't cry,' I tell her. 'Everything will be OK.' Then I go back into the kitchen with my picture. Lissa and Kaydee are sitting at the table with a milkshake each. There are three candles in the middle, and their faces, with the make-up on, look like film stars.

'Want a milkshake, Darby?' Kaydee asks.

'Yeah,' I say.

'Yes please,' Kaydee reminds me.

'Yes please,' I say, and then I remember. 'Thank you for the picture, Lissa.'

She smiles at me. 'No probs.'

I yawn suddenly, which is funny because I went to sleep on the floor of the sitting room earlier and I didn't think I was tired.

Kaydee makes me a strawberry milkshake and she and Lissa talk about this TV show all their friends at school are watching. Kaydee and Lissa think it's a really stupid show and they can't understand why their friends like it. But they've both been pretending they're into it, so that they feel part of the group. I get it. I like feeling part of a group too.

I drink my pink milk and yawn again. 'Go to bed, Darby,' says Kaydee, and she gives me a hug. I hug her back.

'We should clean her face first,' says Lissa.

'No!' I say. 'No, I want it to stay on!'

Kaydee laughs. 'It'll get all over your pillow, and you'll look a right mess in the morning.'

'I don't care,' I say.

Lissa shrugs, but she's smiling. 'Suit yourself.'

I go round to the other side of the table and I hold out my arms to Lissa. She stares at me for a moment. I feel uncertain. Did I do it wrong? But then she gets up from her chair and steps forward, and I hug her. Her body doesn't bend like Kaydee's. Her arms do sort of the right thing but they only bend at the elbow; it's like the top part of her arm is stuck to her side. But it's still a hug, and she says quietly, 'Thanks, Darby. Night night.'

'Night night,' I say, and I take a torch and my picture and go upstairs. I am not scared of the dark this evening, because I am a princess living in a castle where they don't have electric light anyway.

In my room, before I can change my mind, I get down on the floor and reach under my bed for Georgie. She is a bit dusty and fluffy, but I brush her off and put her into my bed. Then I go to the loo and put my pyjamas on and get into bed. I shine the torch onto Lissa's drawing, which is propped up against my laptop. I look like Queen Darby. Then I point the torch straight upwards and write letters on the ceiling with the light:

D-A-R-B-Y

G-E-O-R-G-I-E

K-A-Y-D-E-E

After a moment, I do L-I-S-S-A too.

Then my eyes close, and I fall asleep with the torch still on.

I sleep all night, even when the wind picks up

again and the metal can starts to scrape along the wall. When I wake, I remember exactly why today is going to be the best day ever.

It's the day of the chocolate hunt.

Chapter 19

I have a shower because it's such an important occasion – or at least I try to, but the water stays freezing cold. 'Darby, is that you?' Mum calls through the door. 'The shower's electric, love. The power's still off. You won't get any hot water that way. Have a bath instead.'

I hate baths. So I call back, 'OK!' and don't bother. I look at myself in the mirror and get a shock. I'd forgotten I went to bed with all my make-up on. Despite what Lissa and Kaydee said, it doesn't look too bad. There are smudgy marks under my eyes, so I wipe them with a flannel. The rest of it looks fine, and I like the way the glittery eyeshadow has sprinkled itself over my cheeks. I look all sparkly.

I *feel* sparkly too. It's the chocolate hunt! I dash back to my room, throw my clothes on and go downstairs.

Mum is in the kitchen, chopping vegetables. A big casserole dish sits on the side by the Aga. 'You're up early,' she says with a smile, though her eyes look tired. 'Oh, Darby, didn't you wash your face before you went to bed?' She gives a half-laugh.

'It's the chocolate hunt,' I say.

Her mouth opens slightly, and her eyes widen. 'Oh – oh yes, so it is.' She smiles. 'Do you know, I'd completely forgotten.'

She's *forgotten*?!

'I want to do it,' I tell her, just in case she isn't completely clear.

'I know, sweetheart. It's – I'll make it happen, all right? I just don't know quite when. And your dad won't be able to come, I don't suppose. He's going to be tied up all day.'

'But it only takes ten minutes,' I say. There is a funny feeling in my tummy, like something is wriggling around in there. 'He can come and do it and then go back to work.'

Mum hesitates. Then she says, 'I'll see what I can do, Darby. I can't promise. Have you seen what it's like out there?'

I look out of the window. The wind is still buffeting the trees, and now it's spitting with rain too. It's a strange way to talk about rain, spitting. There's a teacher at school who spits when he talks. It's disgusting and no one wants to sit at the front in his lessons in case they get spit on them. If the rain is spitting, who is doing the spitting?

'Darby.' Mum waves a hand in front of my face. 'Darby, hello? Did you want some breakfast?'

Chapter 20

Kaydee and Lissa come down late for breakfast, bringing the baskets with them, and I smile. 'Don't worry,' Kaydee says, 'we didn't forget.' She gives me a big hug. Then I give Lissa a hug too, which surprises her but she does that sort of stiff-arm hug back. Maybe in her family they don't know how to do hugs properly. We should teach her.

Mum has put the casserole in the Aga and gone to her study, and I am playing Pairs with some Disney cards. I've got my iPod on, but when Kaydee and Lissa come in, I switch it off.

'I can't believe we're having to survive without social media,' Lissa says. 'Everyone must think we're dead.'

'Sorry,' says Kaydee. 'We live in such a black spot. Without the Wi-Fi, we've got nothing. It's practically medieval.'

There's a bang at the back door and the sound of footsteps. A young man appears in the doorway. It's Gregor, Monica's son. He's eighteen and he has dark hair and eyes, and is very tall. He's lived here on the farm with his mum for three years, so we see him quite a lot. I like Gregor very much. He can play lots of Beatles songs on guitar, and in the summer, when we have barbecues for all the workers, he plays and sings. Monica has a great voice too, and usually there are other people who can play instruments, so they make a band. Gregor has very white teeth, and he smiles a lot. Monica says he is a hard worker but spends too much time chatting up girls.

Gregor smiles at me now, and the smile gets even wider when he sees Kaydee and Lissa. 'Well, good morning, girls,' he says. He has an accent because he's not from this country. 'Suddenly the day is so much brighter.' He puts his hand on his chest and nods at us. 'Good morning, Darby, good morning, Kaydee, and good morning . . .?'

'Lissa,' says Kaydee. She looks as if she's trying not to smile.

'Lissa,' says Gregor. 'Melissa, Greek for honeybee.'

'Wow,' I say. 'I didn't know that.'

Lissa laughs. 'Yeah, that's right.'

131

Gregor is really clever. When he's not working on the farm, he does lots of studying. He's passed lots of exams and he wants to have a degree and his own business one day. I think he should be a pop star. Sometimes I imagine me and Gregor forming our own band, going on TV and making records. Kaydee could design the costumes and Mum could manage us because she's got a maths brain and she does all the money for the farm, so managing a band on tour would be easy.

'Were you looking for Mum?' Kaydee asks. 'She's in her study.'

Gregor looks hurt. 'You would send me away so soon? But then the skies will go dark.'

'The skies are already dark,' says Lissa.

'Not in here,' says Gregor, and smiles again.

'We're doing the chocolate hunt today,' I tell him.

'Ah! It comes round so quickly,' says Gregor. 'How many will you collect this year?'

'Forty,' I say. 'Because last year I got thirty-nine.'

'That wasn't last year,' says Kaydee. 'Last year you only got about twelve, and I had to give you half of mine.'

'I got thirty-nine,' I say obstinately, 'and your jumper got caught on a bramble and it was ruined.'

Kaydee stares at me for a moment and then laughs. 'That was about five years ago, Darby!'

I hear a door shut upstairs, and Olly comes thumping down. He passes Gregor in the doorway and they nod at each other. 'All right?'

Olly goes straight to the cupboard to find cereal.

'Will you all be playing the chocolate hunt?' Gregor asks, glancing at Kaydee and Lissa. 'Are spectators allowed? Can we cheer you on?'

Olly snorts as he fills his bowl with cornflakes.

'I can be an excellent cheerleader,' Gregor continues.

'Oh yeah?' asks Lissa. 'Got your own pom-poms?'

He grins at her. 'Specially made. Would you like to see them?'

'I would,' I say. 'I did cheerleading once on holiday. I really like it.'

'Oh, *Darby*,' says Kaydee, and giggles.

'What?' I say. I do like cheerleading. It's even better than dancing.

'Gregor, is that you?' Mum calls from down the hall.

Gregor sighs. 'I am to be torn away from you all.'

Olly and his bowl of cereal pass Gregor in the

doorway just as he is blowing us all a kiss. Olly glances across and says, 'You're wasting your time, mate. Just to let you know.'

Gregor raises his eyebrows and heads off to the study. Olly goes back upstairs.

There's a moment's silence. Kaydee sighs. 'Sorry, Lissa. He's an idiot.'

I'm indignant. 'Gregor isn't an idiot. He's a brainbox.'

'Olly, not Gregor.'

'Gregor plays the guitar too,' I say. 'He's really good.'

'I know. I didn't mean him.'

I spot the chocolate baskets on the table. 'I want to do the chocolate hunt. When is it time?'

Kaydee rolls her eyes. 'I'll go and ask Mum.' She heads out of the kitchen.

'Hey, Darby,' Lissa says, 'do you know this clapping game?'

She teaches me which way to put my hands, so that we clap hands together, then our own, then the backs of our hands. There's a rhyme to go with it too. It's *really* hard to learn, and I keep getting it wrong, but Lissa is very patient. Kaydee comes back as we're practising and says, 'Mum's going out to

134

do the chocolates now, Darby,' and I'm concentrating so hard on the clapping that I just say, 'OK.'

'You've got it!' Lissa says eventually, smiling at me. 'Good job!'

'Do it again,' I say.

So we do the rhyme again with the clapping, and I laugh because I get it right three times in a row.

'Wish I had a sister to play this with,' Lissa says.

'Haven't you got one?' I ask.

She shakes her head. 'No brothers or sisters. Just me.'

I think it would be *awful* not to have a sister. Everyone should have a sister. I am suddenly very sad for Lissa because she's all on her own at home, and so I go and put my arms around her.

Lissa is surprised but she laughs. 'What's this for?'

'I can be your sister if you like,' I say, and after a pause she puts her arms around me too. And then Kaydee stands behind me and hugs us and I'm in the middle, like a Darby sandwich. Then Mum comes in from the hall and says, 'Aww, family cuddle,' and joins in, and then Kaydee squeezes just that bit too hard, and I lean into Mum, and then the four of us sort of lose our balance and bump into a chair, and we all laugh.

'Right,' says Mum, 'that's enough of that. I'm going out to do the chocolates. And no peeking from any of you, all right?' She goes to one of the top cupboards and reaches in. Then she says, 'Hmm, that's funny. I could have sworn I had four packets. Where's the last one gone?'

I panic. I know exactly where it went.

'Girls,' says Mum, turning round, 'have any of you taken a packet of these from the cupboard?' She holds one up: the shiny plastic wrapping that holds those tiny foiled balls of deliciousness.

'No,' says Kaydee, and Lissa shakes her head.

'No,' I echo, a little bit too loudly.

Mum looks at me and then shrugs. 'Well, nothing I can do now. We'll just have fewer than usual.' She glances out of the window. 'It's not going to be much fun. It's really blowing a gale out there. Why don't we do it tomorrow instead? The forecast is better.'

Tomorrow?! What is she talking about? 'No! It has to be today! It's always on a Sunday!'

Mum sighs. 'All right. I don't think you'll enjoy it much though.'

136

She goes through to the sitting room and I can hear the patio door sliding open and then shut. A huge draught blows in, and I shiver. I hate being cold. But if it means chocolate, I will put up with it!

I'm so excited I can barely stand still. I run (yes, run!) upstairs and knock on Olly's door. 'Olly! It's the chocolate hunt!'

He grunts, so I shout louder, to make sure he's heard. 'Olly! You have to come down!'

'Seriously, Darby?' comes the shout from inside the room. 'I KNOW. Give me a minute.'

'Oh! All right.' I run to my own room and grab another jumper, pulling it on over my head and getting my sleeves all rucked up underneath.

I rush back down the stairs again. Kaydee calls, 'Don't run, Darby!' which is what Mum always says about coming downstairs. But I'm wearing my glasses and I'm not *that* clumsy!

'Is she finished?' I gasp as I come into the kitchen.

'She's been out there literally two minutes,' says Kaydee sarcastically.

The back door bangs, and Dad comes in. 'Am I in time?' he says. His hair is all tangled and sticking up, and there are lines on his forehead.

I throw myself at him. 'You made it!'

He hugs me back and kisses me on the top of my head. 'Couldn't miss it, could I? Tornado, shmornado. The world could be ending and I'd still be here for the annual chocolate hunt.'

Right now, I feel completely and utterly happy. 'I want my basket,' I say, reaching over to the kitchen table to pick up the green one. 'Oh!' I stop. 'We don't have enough baskets, if Dad's here.'

'Oh, cheers,' says Dad, pretending to look hurt. 'Did you want me to go away again?'

'No!' I say immediately. 'No, don't!'

'It's all right.' Kaydee reaches for the red one. 'Lissa and I will share.'

The patio door slides open, and my heart thumps an extra beat. I rush into the sitting room. Mum staggers in, pushing hair out of her face. 'My goodness,' she says. 'That was a marathon and a half. Sorry, I haven't been very creative with hiding places. They were practically blown out of my hand.'

'It doesn't matter!' I say. 'Can we go?'

'Wait for everyone,' Mum says. She brightens as Dad comes through. 'You made it!'

'How could I not?' he says, smiling back at her. I love my family.

138

Olly arrives too, pulling on a pair of trainers. 'Darby should go last,' he says. 'Cos she's already had a packet.' He sticks out his tongue at me and laughs.

'What?' says Mum. She looks at me.

I feel a bit sick. 'What?' I say back, because I can't think of anything else to say.

'Is that where the missing packet went?' Mum says.

'Darby ate them all,' Olly says with a grin.

'It was a game,' I say. 'It was Olly's idea.'

No way am I going to be blamed for this – no *way*!

'Oh, Darby,' Mum says, with disappointment in her voice. 'And I specifically asked you earlier if you knew what had happened to the other packet. You lied to me.'

'I didn't!' I say.

She shakes her head and sighs. 'Well, then Olly has a point. You can go out last.'

Last?! There won't be any chocolates left!

Chapter 21

My eyes fill with tears. I can't believe it! If I'd known this would happen, I'd never have eaten the chocolates yesterday! 'That's totally unfair!' I protest, but Mum is already saying, 'Ready . . . go!' and the others are piling out of the patio door into the gale.

'Go on, Darby, out you go,' Mum says.

But I stand in the middle of the rug and shake my head. This is not right. I am being blamed for something that was not my fault. It was Olly who stole the packet from the cupboard; Olly who fed them to me.

'Darby, you're missing the hunt,' Mum says.

But I am angry now – angry and hurt and upset, and I can't go out because I am having *too many feelings* and it's stopping me doing anything. I drop my basket on the floor and stamp my foot. 'It wasn't my fault.'

'Darby.' Mum tries to push me out of the door. 'Come on, you're missing it. You've been looking forward to it for months.'

I am rooted to the floor, like a tree. 'No,' I say fiercely. 'No.' And I fold my arms.

There are shrieks from outside as the others are blown by the wind, and in one strong gust I see Lissa fall onto the ground. Kaydee bends to help her up and falls over herself. Olly is so busy laughing at them that he doesn't see Dad carefully working his way round the flowerbeds, picking up the small shiny objects. Dad is winning, but I don't care.

I don't care about the chocolate *at the same time* as caring ALL about it. It's like there are two separate versions of me, pushing at each other so that neither can move.

'Well, *fine*,' Mum suddenly snaps. She throws up her hands. 'If you want to mess it up for yourself, that's your choice, Darby. The hunt is happening, and you're *choosing* not to take part. This is *nothing* to do with me, so don't go blaming me afterwards. Honestly, you go on and on about this flipping hunt for *months*, and then you throw a tantrum on the day – well, I'm not having it.

141

Not today, there's too much else to worry about. We could lose the *farm*, Darby. We could lose *everything*. I refuse to let you blackmail me over some stupid chocolate hunt!' She turns and storms out of the room.

I stand in the middle of the floor, shaking. I didn't hear half of what she shouted at me – it was too quick, and my brain sort of slides around when people are shouting quickly. But I did hear her say the word *stupid*.

Mum called me stupid.

The others come barging into the sitting room, laughing and panting, clothes and hair all over the place. 'I won!' says Dad, holding up his basket.

'I was sabotaged,' complains Kaydee. 'Lissa fell on me!'

'I was blown over!' Lissa exclaims. 'I didn't do it on purpose!'

Then they all notice me. 'Darby! Why're you still in here? Didn't you come out at all?'

And I can't say anything because right now I feel like the most miserable person in the whole world, because I'm stupid *and* I have no chocolate.

'Darby?' Dad puts his arm around me. 'What's happened? Listen, you can share my chocolates – I can't eat this many anyway.' He passes the basket to me.

And then Mum appears in the doorway and her face is as white as the bathroom tiles upstairs, and Juris is at her elbow, and his face is all tight and staring, and Mum says, 'Paul, we've been hit.'

And Dad's arm drops away from my shoulders, and he says, 'How bad?'

Juris says, 'One greenhouse.'

'A whole one?' asks Dad, and he swallows.

Juris nods. 'Looks like it.'

Dad takes a breath, but it catches in his throat. 'Right,' he says, and walks out of the room. Juris follows him. Mum glances at the rest of us and then turns and goes out too.

'What was all that about?' Lissa asks. 'Hit by what?'

'Tornado,' Kaydee says, and she and Olly look at each other. 'A tornado has taken out one of the greenhouses.'

'I don't understand,' says Lissa.

'It means,' says Olly, 'that the glass has smashed and they've lost a whole greenhouse of fruit. It's a lot of money.'

'How much money?' Lissa asks.

Olly shrugs. 'Hundreds of thousands, if you

include the cost of replacing the glass.'

'Oh wow,' says Lissa quietly. 'That's massive.'

Kaydee looks down at the basket she's carrying and makes a face. 'This is all so pointless. Here, Darby.' She holds out the basket to me, and I take it automatically. 'You have it.'

'Yeah, you can have mine too,' Olly says, holding out his. 'A whole greenhouse . . . they're going to be right up against it. Dad was already worried about breaking even this year.'

'Hey.' Lissa reaches out to Kaydee, who looks like she's about to cry. 'Hey, don't worry. I'm sure it won't be as bad as all that.'

Kaydee lets Lissa pull her into a hug. Lissa strokes her hair.

Olly watches, and on his face is an expression I don't understand. He looks sort of ill. He goes out of the room.

'Come on,' Lissa says to Kaydee. 'What are we going to do to keep your spirits up?'

I feel like I am suddenly invisible. I stand with three baskets full of chocolate, all of them mine, and I feel like I have nothing.

Outside the wind howls and batters, and I hate it. I hate everything.

Chapter 22

In the end, Lissa and Kaydee fetch blankets and sit down on the sofa, and Kaydee brings the family copy of *Winnie-the-Pooh* and starts reading it aloud. I don't know what to do, so I sit on a sofa with a blanket too. I love this book. Piglet is my favourite character because he's strong and brave even though he's small and sometimes scared. He's a good friend to Pooh. Piglet just wants everyone to be happy.

After a while Mum comes in, and when she hears Kaydee reading, she smiles. Her eyes are red so I know she's been crying. And even though she shouted and called me stupid, I get off the sofa and go to her and put my arms around her.

Mum hugs me back, and sniffs and rubs my shoulder.

Kaydee is reading about the arrival of Tigger. She stops at the end of a sentence and looks up at Mum. 'Is it bad?' she asks.

Mum nods and sniffs again. 'Go on reading, darling,' she says. 'You do it so beautifully.'

'My mouth's getting dry,' Kaydee says.

'Lissa, why don't you take over?' suggests Mum. 'Just till I've got lunch ready.'

Lissa's mouth opens slightly and she glances at Kaydee. 'Oh . . .' she says slowly. 'Oh, but Kaydee's doing great.'

Kaydee says to her, 'It's OK, Liss.' And then she looks up at Mum and says, 'Lissa's not so good at reading.'

'Oh,' says Mum, sounding a bit sorry. 'I didn't mean to make you feel awkward. Do you have dyslexia? My sister does.'

Aunty Milly has dyslexia? I didn't know that.

'Sort of,' says Lissa. 'I just . . . well, mainly I just never really learned . . . I didn't go to school much when I was younger.'

Mum puts her head on one side as she looks at Lissa. 'It sounds to me,' she says gently, 'as though maybe you've missed out on some important stuff in your life.'

146

Lissa's eyes are suddenly shiny. She looks cross, which confuses me. 'Yeah, maybe.'

'I'll go and finish up the lunch,' Mum says.

'I'll help,' I say, because I still feel bad for the chocolate-hunt disaster, and I want to be with Mum as much as I can. I follow her through to the kitchen.

'That poor girl,' she says in a low voice as she fills the metal kettle and places it on the Aga. 'She's had such a rough ride. Her dad mixed up with drugs and the police; her not going to school. It sounds like her mum hasn't been able to keep control of the situation either. Poor Lissa – some kids miss out on the things you really need.'

Mum opens the oven and takes out a joint of meat, which she puts on the side. It smells so good my mouth waters. 'Mm. Good, we just need gravy to go with this, and then we're done.' She looks at me and smiles. 'We're so lucky to have each other – you, me, Kaydee, Dad and Olly. Lissa hasn't had the love and support we have.'

'But now she has,' I say without thinking. 'Kaydee loves her.'

Mum smiles at me. 'Friendships can be very close. I'm glad you don't seem to mind as much as you did.' She reaches out to stroke my cheek. 'It's a very mature thing, to accept that your sister has a best friend.'

'I don't mind *now*,' I say. 'I'm going to be their bridesmaid.'

The hand stroking my cheek stills. 'What?' asks Mum.

'When they get married,' I say. 'I'm going to be their bridesmaid.'

Chapter 23

Mum takes a step backwards, staring at me. 'What are you talking about, Darby? When who gets married?'

'Kaydee and Lissa,' I say. 'They love each other.'

And then I remember. 'Oh no! I wasn't supposed to tell!'

'Kaydee and Lissa?' Mum repeats. She takes a step towards me again. 'Darby, you need to be very clear on this. What exactly is going on?'

I am looking at the floor and biting my lip and trying to put my hands in my pockets, except I don't have any pockets. 'I'm not supposed to tell.'

She pauses and then says more gently. 'Darby, you know how sometimes you get fantasy mixed up with reality? Like when we watch a TV drama and you think it's real? Do you think maybe this is one of those times?'

I remember . . .

. . . when I watched *The Lion King* for the first time, I got up to go to the toilet and missed a bit. When I came back, Simba's father was dead, killed by wildebeests. I was sure, absolutely sure, that if I hadn't left the room at that particular moment, he wouldn't have died. It was my fault that Mufasa died; my fault that Simba didn't have a dad. No matter how much Mum and Dad tried to tell me otherwise, and Kaydee rewound the film to show me it would happen over and over again . . . I didn't accept any of it. It was my fault. I killed Mufasa.

I know better now, of course. It was Scar. He sent the hyenas to chase the wildebeests into the gorge so that they would trample Mufasa. And no matter how many times you watch it, the same thing happens. So it couldn't be me. And yet . . . some small part of me still feels guilty.

I say nothing, and the kettle whistles. Mum turns to take it off the Aga, and then says to me, 'This is just one of your fantasies, isn't it, Darby? I know you'd love to be a bridesmaid. You're inventing a wedding.'

'No!' I cry, insulted. 'I haven't invented this! Kaydee and Lissa are in love and I saw them kissing and they're going to be together forever.'

'Ouch!' Mum has spilled some hot water on herself. She bangs down the kettle and heads to the sink, where she sticks her hand under the cold tap. Her face is red and her eyes are shiny.

Kaydee appears in the doorway. 'Are you OK? What's happened?'

Mum turns on her and spits out, 'Are you and Lissa in a relationship?'

'Uh . . .' Kaydee's eyes open wide and she glances at me.

'Don't look at her, look at me!' Mum shouts. I don't know why she's angry. 'Darby says she saw the two of you kissing. Is it true?'

Kaydee turns very red. 'That's none of your business,' she snaps.

'It *is* my business,' Mum says. 'You're my daughter, I have a *right* to know about these things.'

'It's my life, Mum,' snarls Kaydee. 'My decision. I can kiss whoever I like.'

'You're only sixteen,' Mum says. 'You're far too young to know anything.' She cradles her hand under the running water and presses her lips together tightly.

'*What?!*' Kaydee's voice is incredulous – and loud. I clap my hands over my ears. 'I'm old enough to have a *baby* if I want to! I could get *married*!'

'Not without my permission!' shouts Mum.

Tears fill my eyes. They're shouting. I can't bear it. It feels like Kaydee and Mum's shouting is filling the whole house. Even if I went to my room, I would hear them. I run into the hall, through the utility room, out of the back door, along the path, and onto the track that surrounds the site.

The wind is howling, and it dries the tears on my face. The noise out here drowns out the noise from the kitchen.

I stand outside, staring at the big greenhouse in front of me. It wasn't this one that was damaged. I wonder which one was. It shouldn't take long to find it – all the greenhouses are on this site.

I set off to the left, following the track. Past the caravans where our pickers live in the summer –

they'll be arriving in another couple of weeks. Past the shower block, past the shed where all the washing machines and tumble dryers are. Past the big shed where we have barbecue parties and Gregor plays the guitar. On my right I have passed two of the four greenhouses, their air vents jammed open above. At the end of greenhouse number three, the generator stands silent. It's still not working. The strawberry plants aren't getting what they need.

At greenhouse number four, I stop because I have found it. Down the far end, I can see Dad standing with Juris and Monica. Gregor is there too, and some others.

I stand and watch and, as I do, the wind drops suddenly. My ears feel funny: there was a lot of noise and now there isn't, like when you jump into a swimming pool and go underwater (which I don't like doing). It makes the rest of my senses feel wobbly. My glasses are smeary, so the world looks out of focus. I take them off and wipe them on my top. When I put them back on, everything looks much brighter, and I realise the sun has come out too. The greenhouse is lit up, bright white shining off its panes. I walk towards it, slowly. I tilt my head to one side and then the other, seeing how the reflection changes. Up ahead are the panes that smashed – the pieces lie glittering on the grass. I can see into the greenhouse too, and there are the plants, green fruits heavy and ripening, sparkling with tiny shards.

They look so beautiful, and so deadly.

I remember . . .

. . . a teacher at school. She was young and pretty, with long black hair and dark skin and brown eyes lined in black. Her name was Miss Morris, and she had a lovely smile. On the first day she came to our classroom, I just sat and stared at her. I'd never seen anyone so beautiful. She had a soft voice and she really listened. I had reading with her once a week, and that first time I rushed to meet her, bringing my book. She smiled at me and we sat down together. 'This is a nice, easy book,' she commented, looking at the one I had brought.

I didn't think it was that easy, but I smiled at her anyway.

'Off you go then.'

I started to read. After a few moments, she stopped me. 'Darby, I can't understand what you're saying. You need to speak more clearly.'

I tried again. After three sentences, she asked me to

repeat a word. And then I had to do it again. 'Ree-a-lyze', she said slowly.

When I had said it four times, she let me move on to the next word. But I'd forgotten what the sentence was about, so I had to go back to the start. And this time she sighed and shook her head when I got to the word 'realise'.

She stopped me often, asking me to say words again, and then she said I shouldn't follow the words with my finger; that only little children did that. So I tried to read without using my finger, but the words jumped around on the page and I got lost.

Miss Morris smiled that beautiful smile at me, and I felt that she understood the problem. And then she said, 'You're not concentrating, Darby. You have to focus', and it was like being stung by a beautiful princess.

She spoke kindly and with a smile, like she was being helpful and friendly. But everything she said made me feel bad, like I wasn't trying hard enough, or that I was stupid.

I went back to my lesson feeling very confused and miserable. Because it was the first time that I had met something beautiful on the outside that wasn't beautiful on the inside, and I couldn't understand it.

Chapter 24

'Darby!' Dad is running towards me, sprinting over the glittering grass. 'Darby, get back!'

I blink, taking a step backwards out of surprise.

'Didn't you see all the glass?' he says.

'Yes,' I say. 'It's pretty. And awful.'

'It's awful all right.' Dad moves me further away from the glass. 'I don't know, Darby. Sometimes I wonder why we do this.'

'Because people like strawberries,' I say.

He stares at me for a moment, and then all the worry lines across his forehead disappear, and he laughs. He laughs quite a lot, more than I was expecting, and so I laugh too. I must have made a good joke to make Dad laugh so much.

He pulls me to him and hugs me very tightly. My glasses get squashed against my nose, but I don't mind. I hug him back and breathe in his

Dad-smell. Everyone has their own smell. Dad's is like earth and oil and grass and hard work. 'Oh, Darby,' he says, with a chuckle. 'What would we do without you, eh?'

'You would be in a terrible mess,' I tell him, and that just makes him laugh even more.

He squeezes me again and then says, 'You'd better go back, sweetheart. I'm sorry that the hunt this morning didn't go right. Maybe we should put all the chocolates back in the garden and do it again.'

This is a brilliant idea! 'Yeah!' I say. 'I'll go and ask Mum!'

I run back to the house, bursting with excitement. I run through the utility room to the kitchen. Mum is standing by the Aga, carving the joint of meat. 'Mum!' I call. 'Mum, I've had a brilliant idea!'

She jumps a bit and blinks. 'Darby! What . . .? What is it?'

'We can do the chocolate hunt again!' I say. This solves everything – it puts right the wrong hunt this morning. 'After lunch! You can put all the chocolates back in the garden, and we can do it again!'

Mum turns to look at me, and her face is all

blotchy. I am surprised, and then I remember the argument with Kaydee. And Mum's burnt hand, which is all wrapped in kitchen roll.

'I don't think we can do that,' Mum says quietly.

'Why not?'

'Darby! Just . . . Just leave it, OK? I can't . . . think about that right now.' She turns back to the joint of meat. 'I have to get the lunch on the table, and the potatoes are half burned already.'

'I'll help,' I say, feeling bad that she's stressed. I get the cutlery and put it on the table and then get water glasses and fill a jug.

Mum doesn't say anything else while she's carving the meat, but then she gets the plates out and starts dishing up. 'Can you . . . call the others?' she says in a quiet voice.

I go to the stairs and call up, 'Kaydee, Lissa, Olly! Lunchtime!'

I hear a grunt from Olly. He trudges down the stairs, his hair all sticking up. 'I am so sick of the power being off,' he grumbles. 'It's almost enough to make me go for a run, just for something to do.'

'The sun is out,' I say.

He glances out of the window. 'Oh yeah. We

could play football later. You want to?'

'I want to do the chocolate hunt again,' I tell him. 'Dad said we could put all the chocolates back in the garden and do it again, properly this time.'

He laughs and shakes his head, sitting down at the table. 'You're a nutter.'

'I'm not!'

Mum brings a plate of food over to the table. 'Here you go,' she says, putting it in front of him.

'What did you do to your hand?' he asks.

'Oh, nothing,' she says. 'Burnt it a bit with some hot water.'

'You shouldn't put that on it,' Olly says. 'It'll stick. We did it in first aid. You're supposed to put cling film on it. I think.'

'I don't have time now,' Mum says. 'Isn't your sister coming down?' she adds to me.

'I don't know,' I reply.

Mum goes to the hallway and calls up, her voice strained. 'Kaydee! Lissa! Lunch is on the table!'

She comes back into the kitchen and puts a plate of food in front of me. I realise I am *starving*! I dig in straight away, and it's only when I've eaten half of what's on my plate that Lissa comes into the kitchen. She stands in the doorway, looking awkward. 'Um . . .' she says.

'Sit down, Lissa,' says Mum. 'I cooked you some vegetarian sausages instead of the beef.'

'Oh. Thanks. Um . . .' Lissa sits down next to me.

'Where's Kaydee?'

'She . . . er . . . She's not coming down.' Lissa looks at the table while she says this.

There's a silence.

Olly glances from Lissa to Mum and back again. 'What's going on?'

Mum says, 'It's nothing.'

I look at Lissa. 'We're going to do the chocolate hunt again after lunch,' I say. 'Do it properly this time.'

She tries to smile at me, but her face is tight and pale, and it's not a good smile. Mum puts a plate of food in front of her, but Lissa just stares at it as if she's not sure what to do.

'The greenhouse is all glass everywhere,' I say.

'I hope you didn't go near it,' Mum says, getting herself a plate and sitting down at the end of the table.

'So can we do the chocolate hunt again?' I ask.

161

'I don't think so,' Mum says. 'Once is enough.'

'Is Dad coming in for lunch?' Olly says, looking at the cutlery.

'I doubt it,' Mum says. And then she clamps her mouth shut for a moment, like she's about to cry.

Lissa shifts on her chair and pokes at a sausage with her fork.

Olly stares around the table. 'Wow, I know we're a dysfunctional family, but this is a whole other level. What's going on?'

Mum just shakes her head, and then makes a kind of sob and gets up and goes to get a tea towel, which she presses to her face.

Lissa says very quietly, 'I'm not very hungry,' gets up, and makes a dash for the stairs.

I remember . . .

. . . the day Mum and Dad bought the kitchen table. It was a lot bigger than the one we had before.

When the delivery lorry came, the writing on the side said, 'DELIVERS ON TIME ON QUALITY ON THE MONEY' and Dad made a twisty shape with his mouth and said the van was two days late and the table hadn't been cheap, so that was two out of the three already wrong.

There were two delivery men and they wore checked shirts and jeans, and one of them stared at me quite a lot and offered me some chewing gum. Then he laughed like it was a joke, though I wasn't sure why. The other one had a friendly face and a terrible cough. I saw Mum sidling out of the way when he came past in case he coughed germs on her.

The two men got the table out of the back of the lorry and onto the ground. 'There you go,' said Chewing Gum Man. 'Nice bit of furniture, in't it?'

We all stared at the table. Even I could see that it was far too wide to fit through the front door.

Mum said, 'I thought . . . I mean . . . How are you going to get it into the kitchen?'

'Not our problem, love,' said Chewing Gum Man. 'We only have to deliver it. Here we are. Here it is. Sign here.' He held out a form and a pen. To Dad.

'Oi,' said Mum. 'I ordered it. It's my name on the slip.' She snatched the form from Chewing Gum Man. Then she read it very carefully, including the small print at the bottom.

'Women, eh?' said Coughing Man, grinning at Dad and rolling his eyes.

'Women,' said Dad. 'Without them, this business would collapse.'

Coughing Man looked a little embarrassed. He coughed.

Mum sighed and said, 'It does say they only have to deliver to the driveway, not into the house.' She signed the form, adding, 'I think it's a cheek.'

Coughing Man and Chewing Gum Man got back into their lorry and waved goodbye, though they didn't look at Mum again.

Mum and Dad stared at the table, sitting in the middle of the stony track. 'We'll have to take its legs off,' said Mum. 'I'm sorry. I thought it would come flat-packed.'

Dad grinned. 'Didn't read the small print?'

'Oh, shut up,' she told him, but she was smiling too.

My mum has always been good at solving problems.

Chapter 25

When I come out of my remembering, Lissa has gone and Olly is finishing his lunch. Mum is nowhere to be seen. The leftover meat, potatoes and vegetables are gently steaming on the side by the Aga. I finish up the rest of my food. Olly pushes his plate back and then puts his head in his hands. 'Why is everyone so dumb?' he groans.

'I'm not dumb,' I say, indignant.

'I'm not talking about you,' Olly says. 'I'm talking about Kaydee. What a waste.'

'A waste of what?' I scrape my fork across the plate to get up all the gravy.

'A waste of *herself*.' He thumps the table. 'She's fit – she could have any boy she wanted. What's she doing with a *girl*?'

I shrug. 'I dunno.'

Olly goes on. 'She's got all the boys at school

falling at her feet. She doesn't even *notice* them.'

I stare at him. He seems awfully worked up about this.

He sees me staring, and his face goes very red. 'What? I'm just saying, that's all. Plenty of boys would treat her well; plenty of them would be proud to have her as a girlfriend. But no – she has to decide she prefers girls.' He throws up his hands. 'Never mind those of us who've been . . .' He stops talking.

'Been what?' I ask. I get confused when people don't finish their sentences.

'Nothing,' he says. 'Forget it, Darby. Forget all of it.'

'Lissa is nice,' I say. 'Kaydee's going to marry her and they're going to live happily ever after.'

'Oh, don't be stupid, she's not going to marry Lissa,' Olly says. 'She's just . . . I don't know *what* she's doing. It must be a phase. She'll come round to boys in the end.'

A small sound makes me look up.

Kaydee is standing in the doorway.

Chapter 26

Olly and Kaydee look at each other, and in Kaydee's eyes there's something like fire. Not actual fire, but she's staring very, very hard, like she could shoot through him with lasers. The edges of her eyelids are pink and wet.

Then I miss a bit, because the next time I connect with the room, Kaydee has gone and Olly is sitting with his head in his hands. Then he thumps the table again and says a rude word, very loudly, and then he stands up so suddenly that his chair makes a horrible squeaking sound on the floor.

He leaves, and I hear his footsteps go out through the utility room. And then, like a miracle, there's a *phtoo* and the microwave clock lights up, flashing 00:00, and the radio comes on.

'Electricity!' I say joyfully. Now I can plug in my laptop and watch dance videos!

I run upstairs to my room. I have missed my dancing and singing so much!

My laptop boots up and I load one of my favourite songs. It's by an old band called S Club 7. They have really good dance routines that aren't too hard to learn. I like 'Bring It All Back', and when that one has finished, I do it again because I missed a few steps. I have a pretend microphone that Mum bought me from the pound shop. It doesn't plug into anything, but it's really good to sing into.

It's late in the day when Mum comes knocking on my door. 'You hungry?' she asks.

I am red-faced and sweaty from the dancing, but I feel *great*. 'Mum, let me show you this one,' I say, and I put on a music video really loud. Then I do all the moves perfectly.

She smiles at me. 'That's brilliant, Darby, well done you.' She gives me a hug. 'My little star. Going to set the world on fire.'

'Yeah!' I say. 'On TV, that's where I'm going to be. And in films. And in a band.'

She cups my face in her hands. 'You can be anything you want to be, Darby. Don't let anyone tell you different.'

'I won't,' I say.

'Now, come on. It's dinner time.'

To my surprise, everyone is there: Dad, Kaydee, Lissa and Olly – and me and Mum of course. Even Pike and Marmite have come in, cosying up to Bramble in his basket. It's nice – the whole table is full of people. I sit down next to Olly. There's jacket potatoes and cold meats and cheese and hummus and tomatoes and cucumber and all kinds of things. I push the bowl of tomatoes away from me – ew.

'So, Darby,' says Dad, 'you been dancing? I heard thumping around up there.'

'She's done some fantastic routines,' Mum says with a smile. 'I popped in on her a couple of times this afternoon and she was totally engrossed.'

'I'm not gross!' I protest.

Mum laughs. '*En*grossed. It means you were completely focused on your dancing. You didn't even notice me peeking in through the doorway.'

'What's everyone else been doing?' Dad asks, though his voice sounds croaky. I look at him.

'Have you got a sore throat?' I ask.

He coughs. 'No. No, I'm fine.' He turns to Olly. 'What you been up to?'

Olly shrugs. 'Video games.'

'Kaydee? Lissa?' Dad says.

Kaydee says, 'Chatting.' Lissa glances at her and says nothing.

'Can you pass the ham?' asks Mum. Her voice sounds funny too.

'How's the greenhouse?' Kaydee asks Dad.

He sighs. 'Gone. I mean, we've lost all the fruit inside. The other three houses are fine. Tornadoes are so specific; it's baffling.' He shakes his head. 'But at least the power is back on, and the vents are operating properly, and the irrigation system too. So, looks like we've saved the rest of the crop.'

'What about the polytunnels?' Mum asks.

Dad winces. 'Yeah, they're not so good. Should have held off on skinning them. More money.'

I tune out and concentrate on my food. Everyone is behaving normally, eating and passing things. Mum and Dad are talking about the farm, but Mum's eyes keep flicking to Kaydee and Lissa. Something feels wrong.

I look at Lissa carefully. Underneath the make-up and everything, she's really quite pretty. Not as pretty as Kaydee, of course. But she was kind to me when she did my makeover, and she drew an amazing portrait of me, and I feel sorry for her because her dad's in prison and she hasn't had a nice time.

Then I think something else: I'm not jealous of Kaydee and Lissa. Lissa isn't Kaydee's sister. I am. Kaydee will never have another sister. She can have a girlfriend, but that's not the same thing. Kaydee will love her in a different way than she loves me.

'Darby?' Mum is staring at me. 'You all right?'

'Yeah,' I say. I realise everyone is staring at me.

'You've got a huge goofy smile on your face,' says Dad, grinning in response. 'Are you thinking of something that makes you happy?'

'Yeah,' I say.

'Care to share?' he suggests.

But how can I tell them what I've been thinking? The thoughts are right there in my head, but I'm not so good at putting them into words. Finding the right words is hard, and I might get it wrong, and I don't really know how to start . . . so I shrug and say, 'I dunno.'

I remember . . .

. . . when Kaydee told me she was going to walk to a friend's house, because her friend had loads of plums in their garden and she wanted help to pick them and Kaydee loves plums, so she set off to her friend's house.

And Mum came in and asked, 'Where's Kaydee?' and I didn't know how to start my answer because should I start with plums or Kaydee or her friend or the walking? So I shrugged and said, 'Dunno,' which wasn't true but was easier than trying to explain.

And Mum got very agitated and went all round the house calling, and then she phoned Dad, and then she went out. I played a game on my tablet which was all about putting colours into boxes.

And much, much later, Kaydee came home with a bag full of plums, and Mum grabbed her and hugged her really hard and shouted at her that no one had known where she was and she mustn't ever go off without telling someone.

And Kaydee looked at me and said, 'But I told Darby where I was going.'

And then everyone was cross with me.

Chapter 27

It's when we're clearing away that it happens. 'Kaydee,' says Mum in a cheerful voice, 'I think maybe we should let Lissa get a good night's sleep tonight, as she'll be going home tomorrow. You could sleep in Darby's room.'

I am surprised but also very excited. 'Yes!' I say. 'Cool idea!'

Kaydee's face is still and tight, like she's forgotten how to move the muscles in it. 'Why?' she asks.

Olly is clearing plates into the dishwasher, but he keeps looking at Kaydee, so I know he's listening.

'I just think it would be best,' Mum says in a low voice.

'Best for who?' Kaydee demands, and *not* in a low voice.

'Do I really have to spell it out?' Mum says.

Dad interrupts. 'Is everything OK? Ruth, is there a problem?'

Mum takes a deep breath and says, 'I just think . . . they shouldn't share a room.'

Dad looks completely baffled. 'Kaydee and Lissa?' he says, his forehead creasing into lines. 'Why not?'

'Yeah, Mum, *why not*?' Kaydee's eyes are doing that fierce burning thing again.

'What's all this about?' Dad asks.

'If it were a boy staying over, we wouldn't let him share her room, would we?' Mum asks.

'No . . .' says Dad slowly. 'I guess not. But it's not a boy. It's her best friend.'

'She doesn't want them sharing a *bed*, Dad,' Olly butts in. 'How dense can you be?'

There's a sort of silence, and Dad's face goes through a combination of expressions. He looks confused, and then he looks like he's seen a ghost (Max at school says he's seen a ghost and it wasn't in a white sheet or anything – it looked like a normal person only it walked through a wall) and then his lips press together and I think maybe he is angry. 'Kaydee,' he says, and his voice is thin and nervous, 'is this . . . what is this?'

'What do you mean?' Kaydee says, and her eyes

are very bright and shiny. Lissa comes to stand next to her and holds her hand.

'Have you . . .?' Dad doesn't know what to say next. 'Is this . . .? Are you . . .?'

Olly throws up his hands. 'Good *grief*, Dad.' Then he leaves the room.

'What if I am?' counters Kaydee.

'It's not . . .' Mum starts. Then she stops and starts again. 'Darling, we don't mind who or how you are or anything. It's not a big deal.'

'Really?' says Kaydee. 'Because it *sounds* like it's a big deal.'

'I'm just . . . disappointed for you,' Mum says. 'Life is going to be so much harder for you if you take this route.'

I'm not quite sure what she's talking about. Is Kaydee going away? Because nobody told me.

'It's not a *choice*,' Kaydee says, and I can see Lissa's hand tighten around hers. 'It's who I *am*.'

Oh! She's talking about loving Lissa, a girl, not a boy. I go and stand on Kaydee's other side and take her other hand. 'I don't mind,' I say loudly. 'I love Kaydee and I want her to be happy.'

'Oh, Darby, it's not as simple as that,' Mum says, as though I'm stupid.

'Yes, it is,' I say. But I am scared. *No one* in this room is happy at this moment.

'You don't understand,' Mum says, and I think it's the first time *ever* she's said that to me.

It makes me very angry. 'Yes, I do,' I say. 'Kaydee and Lissa love each other.'

Dad's eyes go wide in shock. 'What?'

'They love each other and they're going to get married and I'm going to be their bridesmaid,' I say.

Now Kaydee and Lissa go, '*What?!*'

'People who love each other should be together,' I go on, despite the fact that Kaydee and Lissa are also now talking. 'There's too much bad stuff in the world. Wars and bullying. And . . .' I try to think, but it's hard when there's other noise. 'And animal cruelty. People should have things that make them happy, like dancing and singing and strawberries. And people they love . . .' I stop because no one is listening to me. They're all talking over each other, and I am really cross because what I just said was very important and no one heard it.

The noise is too much, so I let go of Kaydee's hand and put both my hands over my ears and screw up my face. 'Stop it, stop it, stop it!' I shout.

Mum storms out of the room, and Dad stands for a moment looking like he doesn't know what to do. Then he too goes out of the room.

Kaydee and Lissa are crying, and that makes me unhappy. Kaydee says to Lissa in an angry voice, 'I can't believe they're taking it like this! After everything Mum's always said.'

Lissa's hands are trembling. 'I should sleep downstairs,' she says.

'What?' says Kaydee. 'No!'

'I can't . . .' Lissa sounds all wobbly. 'I don't . . . Look, it's their house. I should do what they say.'

'It's my house too,' says Kaydee. 'And I say we have to stick together on this. We talked about it before, remember?'

'But they're so angry,' Lissa says weakly. 'They want you to be happy.'

Kaydee turns on her fiercely. '*You've* made me happier than I've *ever* been! The way you laugh, the way you listen and think, and what you do . . . you're *magic*, you are. And I *won't* be without you. Not now, not *ever*.'

Lissa's eyes are streaming, and I go to put my arms around her, but she's stiff. 'I still think I should sleep downstairs tonight,' she whispers.

Kaydee stares at her, and her mouth opens and closes a couple of times before she manages to say anything. 'Are you . . . are you . . . what are you saying?'

'I don't want people to be angry with me,' Lissa says in a small voice. 'I can't deal with it.'

'But this *matters*.' Kaydee's face is very pale.

'I know it matters,' Lissa says. 'But maybe we're rushing into things. They just want what's best for you. Maybe I'm not it.'

'You're *defending* them,' says Kaydee. 'You're on their side, when you should be on mine!'

'I *am* on your side,' Lissa says, but her voice cracks. 'But I can't fight, Kaydee. I'm not strong like you.'

'This isn't about your dad,' Kaydee snaps. 'This is about *us*.'

I am a bit confused because I don't understand why Kaydee is talking about Lissa's dad.

'I'm sorry,' whispers Lissa, and she looks at the floor.

Kaydee shakes her head, lots of times. 'I can't believe it. You're . . . are you breaking up with me?'

'No!' Lissa says. 'I love you.'

'Well, that's not what it sounds like.' Kaydee's

voice is hardening, like it's turning to stone. 'Fine. Maybe it's better that I found out now. Before I . . . invested too much in you. In us. I'll get you a sleeping bag. You needn't come up to my room at all.' Then she runs out of the room and we hear her feet stomping up the stairs.

Lissa puts her shaking hands over her face. I go to hug her but she turns away. 'Oh, Darby,' she moans, 'why can't I ever stand up for myself? Why do I just run away the minute there's an argument?'

I shrug. 'I dunno.' I am feeling quite tired all of a sudden. There is way too much emotional stuff going on. 'Do you want to listen to some music?' I ask Lissa.

She wipes her eyes and sniffs. 'What?'

'Do you want to listen to my music?'

'Oh.' Lissa makes an attempt at a smile. 'N-no, thanks. That's . . . very sweet of you. I don't feel like it right now.'

There's a thumping noise as something bounces down the stairs. Lissa and I go out into the hallway. A sleeping bag and a pillow are at the bottom of the stairs. A few moments later, Kaydee appears at the top of the stairs and throws down a pair of pyjamas too. 'Your toothbrush is in the bathroom,' she tells Lissa, before turning away and going back to her room.

Lissa picks up all the things, biting her lip. I know she is trying not to cry. She drops the pillow on the way to the sitting room, so I pick it up and put it on the sofa in there. 'It's quite a nice room to sleep in,' I tell Lissa. 'The sofa is comfy and there are blankets, and Bramble will come and sit on your feet and keep them warm.'

She nods but doesn't say anything.

'Kaydee loves you,' I say. 'And I love you too. Don't be sad.'

She takes a breath, and then she says, quietly, 'Darby, thank you so much but I'd like to be on my own for a bit, if you don't mind.'

'OK,' I say.

It's still early – far too early to go to bed. But everyone has disappeared. So I go back up to my room and watch a TV show on my laptop.

I hope things are better in the morning.

Chapter 28

In the night, I wake from a nightmare. In it, Kaydee is shouting at me, but although I can hear her, I can't understand the words. And then all this stuff starts coming out of her mouth: sheets, duvets and pillows, one after the other. It all piles up on top of me until I'm buried under a mountain of bedding, and I know she's still shouting but I can't see or hear her any more because I'm completely in the dark. I wake up sweating and frightened, and I've got my head right under the duvet, so it takes me a while to find the way out.

I sit up in bed, trembling. I'm very hot, and my fringe is sticking to my forehead.

I need Georgie. She was in my bed last night; where is she now? I reach around under the duvet, finding nothing. I check under my pillow: nothing. I get out of bed, pull the duvet right off . . . nothing.

Maybe she's back under the bed? I put on my glasses and get on the floor with a torch. I can't see her. I squeeze right under the bed, so I can reach all the way to the wall, but my fingers close on old schoolbooks, dressing-up clothes, balls of fluff.

No Georgie. She's not there.

I sit back, staring. I *had* her yesterday. Didn't I? This weekend feels like it's lasted a very long time.

Then I remember Kaydee's threat. She said if I told Mum about her and Lissa, she'd tear Georgie apart.

I straighten in shock. Has Kaydee taken Georgie? Now I am frightened. She wouldn't do what she said, would she? But I *did* tell; I didn't keep her secret. It was an accident. But what if she's taken Georgie anyway, just like she threatened?

I get to my feet. I will go up to Kaydee's room and beg her to give Georgie back.

I tiptoe across the landing to the stairs that lead up to Kaydee's room. I can hear Olly snoring. I go up the stairs, remembering to avoid the two that creak especially loudly. At the top, I push open the door gently. 'Kaydee,' I whisper. 'Kaydee.'

There's no answer, so I go in. 'Kaydee,' I say again, but then I stop.

The bed is empty. Where is she?

She must have gone downstairs to be with Lissa. I go back down Kaydee's stairs, then the main stairs to the ground floor. I turn right and walk through the kitchen with its ticking clock. Marmite lifts his head and thumps his tail softly on the floor. His eyes gleam. 'Shh,' I tell him, and I go to the door that leads to the sitting room. It is open a little, and I peep through.

Lissa is there on the sofa, sleeping. Bramble snores at her feet.

I glance around the sitting room, but there's no one else there.

Where is my sister?

Chapter 29

I stand in the kitchen for a moment, thinking. Where would Kaydee go? The clock says 4 a.m. She can't be in the bathroom; the light wasn't on. She's not in her bedroom. She's not in the sitting room. She wouldn't be in Olly's room, or Mum and Dad's. Would she be in Mum's study? Seems a bit unlikely, but I check anyway – no Kaydee.

There's only one room left: the utility room. She isn't there, but I do notice two things. Her coat has gone. And so have her boots.

I try the handle of the back door. It's unlocked. Kaydee has gone outside.

Well, if Kaydee has gone out, then I'll have to go too, even though it's dark out there and I hate the dark. I can't go back to bed without Georgie.

There isn't a storm any more, but it won't be warm outside, so I pull on a spare fleece. We always have lots hanging by the door for anyone to borrow. This one is too big for me, but never mind. I put my waterproof coat on over the top, because even though it's not raining, it might be soon. I put my wellies on too, over my bare feet.

Then I pick up a torch and go out of the back door, closing it quietly behind me.

I don't have any particular idea where Kaydee might be, so I start walking round the site. My boots make a faint squishing noise on the damp grass, which is kind of nice to listen to, and it takes my mind off the darkness around me. I swing the torch from side to side as I walk. Kaydee's coat is bright pink with a reflective stripe down each arm, so she should be easy to spot. I don't want to call out because I am passing caravans where people are sleeping. As I pass Monica and Gregor's caravan, I hesitate. Gregor would be a good person to ask for help. But he might be cross if I woke him up, and Monica would go and tell Mum, and then everyone would be cross with me, so I decide not to.

Squish. Squish. Squish. The inside of the wellies feels smooth against my bare feet. I like it. *Squish. Squish.*

I walk all the way round the outside of the

greenhouses, carefully avoiding the broken glass, and find myself back at the start again. I'm a bit surprised. It didn't feel like I'd walked that far. There's no sign of Kaydee.

If she isn't here, she must be somewhere else.

I head down the driveway and out onto the road. Out of habit, I turn left, since that's the direction of the other sites of our farm.

My wellies on the road make a different sound, almost clopping like a pony. I try walking more quickly, and then more slowly. My feet are quite cold, and the inside of the wellies doesn't feel as comfy. I wish I had some socks.

Every now and then I swing the torch around the grass verge and call, quietly, 'Kaydee!' But I don't see her.

A car comes along the road with really bright headlights. I step back onto the verge, trip and sit down heavily, putting my hand straight onto a thistle. 'Oww.' It's the same hand I put in the nettles the other day. It must be my unlucky hand.

The car goes past. What is anyone doing out on the road at this time? Maybe they are a doctor or a vet. Or maybe they're out looking for Kaydee too.

Well, anyway. Can't sit around here all night. I get up, wiping my wet and prickled hand on my coat. It hurts.

I feel a bit cross. Kaydee is annoying me now. Making me tramp around in the middle of the night.

I set off again. The cold creeps up my legs. I can't feel my toes at all now. I'm not really sure I can feel my feet. But they are still working, which is sort of strange really.

I remember . . .

. . . Caoimhe at one of my day clubs. She was in a wheelchair because she'd fallen off a trampoline and broken a bit of her back. She couldn't feel her legs. When we met, she said her name was Keeva. And then one day I saw it written down, and it was completely not spelled like that at all. In fact, I thought it was someone else, but she took the name sticker and stuck it on herself. 'That's not your name,' I said, and she said, 'Yes, it is. It's Irish,' which didn't explain anything.

I keep walking and walking, feeling crosser and crosser with Kaydee as I go. When I find her, I'm going to tell her off for taking Georgie and making me chase after her all through the country.

In a little while the road forks, and I take the right-hand one, crossing the road carefully. There's a pavement here, which is good.

It's not quite so quiet now; the sky is getting lighter and the birds are singing in the trees. Dad calls it the 'dawn chorus' but it's not like a chorus in a song. Birds all sing different tunes. Apart from crows, which don't sing, they croak, like they've got very sore throats. Or are angry. But they're not Angry Birds, because that's a type of computer game.

I'm getting hungry now. A couple more cars go past, and one of them slows, the driver peering at me. My heart speeds up. I have seen news reports about children being kidnapped by people in cars. I walk a bit faster. The car pulls in behind me, and I hear the door open. 'Hey!' calls a man's voice. 'Are you OK? Do you need some help?'

I shake my head without looking back, and I walk even faster.

After a moment, I hear the door slam and the

car drive off. I stop then, breathing heavily, my head all dizzy. I was nearly kidnapped!

I should get off the pavement. I don't want anyone else to see me.

I take the next footpath, which leads down the side of some houses and into fields. Aunty Milly lives down here. Her house is the last one on the left before the fields begin. My tummy rumbles. I could go to Aunty Milly's for breakfast once I've found Kaydee.

I carry on past the house and into the field. I don't really know where I'm going, but Kaydee has to be somewhere, so I'll just keep walking and looking until I find her.

I cross one field and then the next, and I don't need my torch now because the sun is up, and thankfully it's still not raining. I am cold and hungry and I would quite like to sit down and not go any further. But I still haven't found Kaydee, so I keep going, calling for her every now and then, and trying not to trip over the holes in the ground. I am looking down a lot, but then I look up to check I'm going in the right direction and suddenly . . .

There is a deer.

Two deer, in fact. They're just across the field

from me, I don't know how far, but they're close enough that I can see the speckly bits in the fur on their backs. They have delicate heads, and they're both looking at me, their ears twitching a little. They are gorgeous.

I really, really want to stroke them. I bet they're very soft. I fumble in my pockets but I already know that I don't have any food to offer them (otherwise I'd have eaten it). On the ground are tufts of grass, so I bend down slowly and tear up some. My prickled hand is still sore, but I don't care because I am going to bring home two deer to the farm where they can live with us and be my pets. I could have some rabbits and squirrels too, like Snow White.

I walk slowly toward the deer, my handfuls of grass held out in front of me. I don't want to startle them. I know how to talk to animals.

They watch me approach, and they stay perfectly still. And then, just as I think I'm going to actually do it, just as I'm only about ten steps away . . . they run. Leaping over the hedge, higher than my head, on those spindly legs, and then they're gone.

'Oh,' I say out loud, which startles me a bit because everything had been so quiet. I look down at the grass in my hand, and suddenly I'm very, very tired and cold and hungry, and everything is miserable, and I let out a really big shout: 'KAYDEE!!' because it's all I've got left.

And then her voice answers.

'Darby?'

Chapter 30

You know how sometimes you hear things and you're not sure they're real?

That.

I must have imagined her voice. I mean, I was looking for her, wasn't I? So I hit myself on the head, because I am stupid, just like Mum said, and I realise now this has all been a total waste of time. I'll go back to Aunty Milly's and she'll give me breakfast and maybe some socks.

Kaydee's voice comes again. 'Darby, is that you?'

I *didn't* imagine it. 'Kaydee?'

'Darby!' Her voice is stronger. 'Darby, I'm here! Oh God, Darby!'

It sounds close, but I can't see her. 'Where are you?' I call.

'On the other side of the hedge!' she shouts back.

I bend down to look through it, the hedge the

deer have just jumped, and I can see her pink coat through the branches. 'Kaydee! What are you doing there?'

'I fell in a ditch!' she says. 'I've hurt my ankle. And I dropped my phone in a puddle and it won't work. Oh, Darby, I'm so glad to see you!' She starts to cry.

'Don't cry, Kaydee!' I tell her. 'I'm coming to get you.'

I try to push my way through the hedge but it's too thick. The sharp twigs scratch at my face and hands.

'Not here!' Kaydee says, in a wobbly voice. 'There's a cut-through further up.'

I disentangle myself and follow the hedge along until I find the gap. I squeeze through and nearly trip, because on the other side is a shallow ditch. The ground is very squelchy, and I nearly lose one of my wellies in a patch of mud, but I scramble over the ditch and get to my feet again. Kaydee is sitting on the ground a little way off, and I am *so* pleased to see her that I run towards her, which is surprising because I didn't think I had anything left in me to run.

I collapse on the ground next to her, and she

reaches out to hug me and bursts into proper loud sobs, and I cry a bit too because I am very glad I don't have to wander around the fields on my own any more.

When she stops the really loud part of the sobbing, I say, 'Kaydee, where's Georgie?'

She stops crying completely and stares at me. 'What? What do you mean, where's Georgie? How would I know?'

'You took Georgie,' I say.

'No, I didn't. Darby, what are you doing out here all on your own? Where's Mum?'

'At home,' I say. 'I came to find you because of Georgie. I needed her in the night but she wasn't there. And you're the only one who knows where I keep her. You said you'd tear her apart if I told about you and Lissa.'

'Oh, *Darby*,' says my sister. 'Of course I wouldn't do that. I was angry with you. But I'd never do that.'

I am puzzled. 'So you *didn't* take her?'

She shakes her head. 'No.' Then she says, 'Oh my gosh, did you come looking for me because you thought I had Georgie?'

'Yeah,' I say.

Kaydee starts to laugh. She laughs and laughs and laughs and then I start laughing too, even though I don't know why it's funny, and then she reaches out to hug me again and then the laughing slows down and she does that sort of *ohhh* sound people make when they're stopping laughing. 'Brilliant,' she says. 'Brilliant. I can't believe you found me.'

'I didn't,' I say. 'The deer did.'

And it's true, because if I hadn't seen the deer, I wouldn't have crossed the field to this side at all. The public footpath doesn't go this way. 'We need to go home,' I tell her. 'Because I'm hungry.' Also, Kaydee doesn't have Georgie, which means someone else must.

The smile slides off her face. 'I can't.'

'We'll go to Aunty Milly's house,' I say, reaching out to pull her to her feet. 'I'll help you.'

She resists. 'No, I mean I can't go *home*. I'm not welcome there. You saw what Mum and Paul were like over Lissa. Even Olly.'

'But everyone loves you,' I say. 'And Lissa's there.'

Kaydee's eyes fill with tears. 'But she won't stand by me, Darby. She's too scared. You know, her dad used to shout at her all the time when she was little. She could never do anything right. Now she just backs off at the first sign of trouble.'

My tummy rumbles. 'Come on.'

'Mum and Paul took it *really* badly,' Kaydee goes on. 'I'm so angry with them. I thought they were better than that.'

'It's been a bad weekend,' I say, thinking about the chocolate hunt.

'Yeah . . .' says Kaydee slowly. 'I guess it has. But even so . . .'

'They'll get over it,' I say, because this is something I've heard adults say. 'Give them time.'

She stares at me for a moment, and then she starts laughing again.

I'm finding it a bit hard to keep up with whether Kaydee is happy or sad.

'You're brilliant, you are,' she says. 'Where did you hear all that?'

'I dunno,' I reply.

My sister gives me another big hug and whispers into my ear, 'I love you, Darby. You're the best sister in the whole world.'

'I love you too,' I tell her. 'Can we go and get some breakfast?'

Chapter 31

It's very hard to get Kaydee to Aunty Milly's. Not because she doesn't want to go but because she's properly hurt her ankle, and she can't walk on it much. She winces and leans on me a lot, and she's quite a bit taller than me and I'm all tired out, so helping her across the fields is really, really hard.

'I wish I hadn't killed my phone,' Kaydee sighs. 'Water and phones don't mix.'

'You have to put it in the airing cupboard in a cup of flour,' I say.

She giggles. 'Rice, you loon, not flour. If I put it in flour, goodness knows what'd happen to it. Phone cake, probably. Oh, owww, my ankle *really* hurts.'

We have to keep stopping, and I dunno how long it takes us to get to Aunty Milly's but it's ages. 'I woke up in the night and I just couldn't bear to be in the house any longer,' says Kaydee. 'I had to get out. So I started walking. I don't know where I thought I was going really. I just needed to get away. And after a while I thought maybe I could stay with Aunty Milly. But it was still dark, and you can't just go knocking on people's doors in the middle of the night. I couldn't think where else to go – and then I saw a barn across the fields, and I thought I could wait in there because it would be warmer. But I fell in the ditch and couldn't get up, and then my phone wouldn't work.' She stops talking because she's crying again.

I say, 'But it's OK now. I found you, and Aunty Milly will give us breakfast. And maybe some socks.'

Kaydee looks down at my feet and says, 'Oh, Darby, you came out in the middle of the night with no socks on?'

I say, 'It wasn't the middle of the night, it was 4 a.m.'

'I bet you didn't tell anyone where you were going, did you?' Kaydee looks at me like a school-teacher.

'No,' I say. 'I forgot.'

She sighs, and then grimaces as she puts her

poorly foot down. 'I think I might have to go to hospital.'

I look at her in alarm. 'What for?'

'To have my heart examined because it fell in love with a girl, not a boy,' Kaydee says seriously.

I stare at her.

She bursts out laughing. 'For my *foot*, you idiot.'

'Can they examine hearts for falling in love with the wrong people?' I ask.

'No. Get that idea out of your head right now. Oww, oww!'

'We're here,' I say, because it's true. Aunty Milly's house is right in front of us.

'I really, *really* hope she's in,' Kaydee groans as she limps up to the front door.

Chapter 32

Aunty Milly is in, and very surprised to see us standing on her doorstep. Kaydee is at least wearing proper clothes, but I'm still in my nightie and fleece and coat. Her house feels super-warm after being outside, and Aunty Milly fetches me some socks.

'Oh, Darby, look at your poor feet,' Kaydee says. They are all rubbed and sore with blisters. And some of the fluff from inside the boot has got into the blistery bits, which makes them look disgusting.

Aunty Milly is not the fussing sort, which is good because she doesn't ask us lots of questions. Instead she makes us some toast and then gets straight on the phone to Mum and Dad, and within ten minutes they have driven over. Lissa is with them. Kaydee goes red in the face and starts crying, but she can't get up because Aunty Milly has made her sit on the sofa with her foot up and a bag of frozen peas on her ankle.

Lissa stands in the doorway and stares at the floor.

Mum rushes over and gives me a huge hug. 'What on earth did you think you were doing, Darby? You have to stop wandering off without telling anyone!'

I wasn't wandering. I was looking for Kaydee. But instead I say, 'Sorry, Mum,' because it seems like the sort of thing she wants me to say. Then I realise I've got toast crumbs down my front and I try to brush them off before anyone notices.

Dad looks at Kaydee, and I can't work out if he's angry or happy to see her or what. Then he sighs and says, 'I'm glad you're OK.'

'Well, she isn't really,' points out Aunty Milly. 'She needs an X-ray on that ankle. It's swollen up like a balloon.'

'What?' Mum lifts up the bag of peas and gasps. 'Oh, Kaydee! How did you do that?'

'I fell in a ditch,' Kaydee says. Her lip trembles and she adds, 'I'm sorry.'

Mum gives her a big hug, and Dad squeezes her shoulder, and Mum tells her it's fine, they're just glad to have her back.

Kaydee nods, and then she looks at Lissa, but Lissa is still looking at the floor. Then she glances up and her eyes bump into Kaydee's, and Lissa looks away again really quickly. Neither of them says anything.

Dad says, 'We need to get Kaydee to hospital.'

'*You* need to get back to the farm,' Mum says. 'I'll take her. I can drop the three of you back at the house and then go on.'

'I want to come to the hospital,' I say. Then I look at Lissa, standing silent and sad in the doorway, and I say, 'And Lissa wants to come too.'

Lissa bites her lip and nods.

There's a pause. Mum looks at Dad. Dad looks at Kaydee. I look at everyone.

'All right,' says Mum at last. 'But we'll pick up clothes for you first, Darby. You're not going to the hospital in your nightie.'

Chapter 33

I know our hospital well. I had to go quite a few times when I was little. But I haven't been to Accident and Emergency before. In America, they call it the Emergency Room, which isn't a very good name because it's not one room, it's several rooms. The biggest one is the waiting room, which isn't emergency-ish at all, because everyone is just sitting around. We sit down on the seats, and Mum helps Kaydee put her foot up. Kaydee lets out little whimpers when she moves, so it must be hurting her a lot.

Lissa is very, very quiet. In fact, she doesn't say anything at all. I don't know what to say to her, but I think maybe she's sad, so I sit next to her and hold her hand.

We have to wait ages. Mum gets some magazines for us to look at. We sit in a row: Kaydee, Mum, me, Lissa. I let go of Lissa's hand to take a magazine. I like magazines because they're about celebrities, and I love all that stuff. One of my favourite girl singers is in there. I don't read the interview but I look at the pictures of her and some other people dressed up for a party. I like nice clothes. Maybe when I grow up I'll be a model instead of a singer or a dancer.

Mum gets us some snacks and drinks from the vending machines, and then Kaydee says, 'I need a wee.'

Mum helps her off down the corridor.

Lissa puts her head in her hands. I can tell she's sad so I say, 'It's going to be OK.'

She pulls her hands away to say, 'Is it?' There are dark smudges under her eyes from where her make-up has run. 'I don't think it is, Darby. I shouldn't have come. I should get on a bus and go home.' She stands up. Then she says, 'Oh. I didn't bring any money,' and sits down again.

'I don't want you to go,' I say. 'I want you to stay and Kaydee does too.'

She smiles a bit. 'I just don't think I'm strong enough.'

I don't understand. 'What do you mean?'

'Love.' Lissa stares at the wall in front of us, which has a pinboard covered in leaflets. 'It's not enough on its own, Darby. You can love someone with all of your heart and soul, but you have to be strong and brave too. You have to stand up for yourself. You have to say, "This is who I am and what I want, and no one is going to stop me." I just . . . I don't know if I can do that. No matter how much I love Kaydee.' Her eyes fill again. 'I don't know what she sees in me. I'm nothing compared to her. She's so alive, so . . . *bright*, that it burns me to look at her. I was off the rails when we got together. She . . . She keeps me safe, you know?'

I don't understand the bit about the rails, but I nod, because I know what she means about Kaydee being bright. Like the sun.

'She has to help me along all the time, pick me up when I'm down,' Lissa goes on.

'She does that for me too,' I say. Maybe Lissa doesn't know that's what you're supposed to do, because her family isn't like that.

Lissa gives a cross sort of shrug. 'Maybe she's fed up of doing it for me. Maybe she's realised I'm not worth the effort. I wouldn't blame her.'

Lissa wipes her eyes hurriedly, because Mum and Kaydee are coming back from the toilet. But before they reach us, a doctor comes into the waiting room and calls Kaydee's name. So Mum gives us a wave and they head off again.

I remember . . .

. . . being very young. There was a mobile that hung over me – the Very Hungry Caterpillar with all his foods. A plum, a strawberry, a piece of cake, a salami . . . I loved that mobile.

In my memory, there's a face looking down at me, and it's not Mum's. It's Kaydee's. She's smiling at me, and I know, just by the look in her eyes, that she loves me. She doesn't need to say anything. I just know. And I've always known.

Mum says I must have imagined that memory because I was too little to be able to remember back that far. But she's wrong.

I don't know what to say to Lissa because I feel sad for her, so I just hold her hand again. When Kaydee and Mum come back, Mum tells us that the doctors are going to X-ray Kaydee's ankle because they're not sure if it's broken, and that's the only way to tell. We wait some more. I wish I'd brought my iPod. I say this to Lissa, and she pulls out her phone and earphones and we share them. Her music is different from the sort of stuff I usually listen to. You couldn't really dance to it. But it's kind of nice. My eyes droop, and I lean my head on Lissa's shoulder.

When I wake up, Kaydee is back from her X-ray with her foot all bandaged up. It's not broken. Mum says something about ligaments which I don't understand, but I'm glad it's not broken.

We all climb in the car to go home, and I'm getting hungry again. Mum says she'll make us lunch and then I should go back to bed. 'And your mum will be coming to pick you up, Lissa.'

I glance at Lissa. She blinks and looks out of the car window.

Kaydee is in the front seat and she doesn't say anything.

Inside me, something really hurts. I think it's a pain for Kaydee and Lissa.

Lissa said she doesn't think she's good enough for Kaydee because she's not brave or strong.

Brave and strong are good things to be, I know. But does it matter if Lissa isn't brave or strong? When Kaydee is with Lissa, she looks happy. Big-smiling, wide-eyed, *shining* happy. I love anyone who can make her look like that.

I sit up straighter. I am brave. I am strong.

I will fight for Kaydee and Lissa.

Chapter 34

Mum puts Kaydee on the sofa with her foot up. Even though it's not broken, she's not supposed to walk on it for a while. The hospital has given her crutches.

The rest of us have lunch at the kitchen table. Olly asks what happened, and Mum tells him about Kaydee going out in the night and me going after her. I am too busy thinking to listen. I think Olly says, 'Darby, you idiot,' at one point, but I ignore him.

After lunch, Olly says he wants to go into town to meet up with some mates, and Mum agrees to take him. Lissa goes upstairs to pack her things. She looks pale and she still hasn't said anything. I don't think she ate anything either.

It's just me and Mum in the kitchen. I say, 'Mum, I don't want Lissa to go home.'

She gives me a sort of smile and says, 'I know

213

you like her, Darby. It's nice. She's a nice girl.'

'I don't want her to go home,' I say. 'Not when she's sad.'

Mum thinks for a moment and then she says, 'Relationships are complicated, Darby. It's hard to be happy all the time.' She glances at the clock and adds, 'I'm going to nip to the site office and see if your dad needs anything picking up while I'm in town.'

I follow her out of the kitchen, through the hall and out of the back door. I am wearing slippers but I only notice that when I step in a muddy bit. Too late now.

I can't believe it's only a few hours since I was wandering around here in the dark with a torch. The sun is shining again and I expect the broken glass is twinkling in the grass, but Mum doesn't go that way. She goes straight to the site office, where Dad is talking to Juris and looking at the computer. I follow her into the cabin.

'I won't interrupt,' says Mum, which is a thing adults say just before they interrupt. 'I'm off in a minute to take Olly into town. Do you need me to pick anything up?'

Dad blinks for a moment and then says, 'Yes – hang on, I made a note somewhere. There were a couple of things . . .' He digs around in his pockets.

Juris says to me, 'Exciting weekend, eh, Darby?' and smiles.

I say, 'Everything went wrong. And it's *still* going wrong.'

He stops smiling.

'What are you talking about, Darby?' asks Dad, still hunting in his pockets. 'What's gone wrong now?'

'Lissa's going home,' I say. 'And I don't want her to, because Kaydee loves her. And,' I add, 'I want another makeover.'

Dad glances at Mum, and then he looks at Juris for a moment, and then he looks at me and says, 'Shall we have a quick chat?' And Juris goes to the computer, and Dad and Mum and I go back out to the sunshine and the muddy ground.

My slippers are soggy.

'Darby,' Dad says, 'I know it's hard to understand about Kaydee and Lissa.'

'No, it isn't,' I say. 'They were really happy and then you found out they were together and you didn't like it, and now they're sad. And so am I.' I do feel sad. And tired and frustrated. Because it feels like everyone else isn't understanding something that's really kind of easy.

Mum gives a little sigh. 'I didn't handle it well, I know. I've been so worried about the farm – we've come very close to losing everything, sweetheart. I've hardly slept. And then I burned my hand, and . . . I could have managed the situation better. I was scared and in pain. It made me say things I maybe shouldn't have.'

Dad says, 'But, Darby, this isn't as simple as you think. If Kaydee is . . . if she likes girls . . . life will be that much harder for her. People will make her life harder because of it.'

I am really confused. 'But *you* are making it harder.'

'We just want her to be happy,' Mum says.

'But . . . *Lissa* makes her happy.'

'It's more complicated than you think,' Dad tells me.

I am tired and now I'm cross. 'You keep saying that! Don't treat me like I'm stupid! I'm not stupid! You say one thing and then another but it's all rubbish.'

Dad frowns. 'Don't talk to us like that.'

'If you send Lissa home, Kaydee will cry lots and lots,' I say. 'And Lissa will cry too. And *I* will cry, and then I will *never talk to you again*.' I fold my arms.

Mum reaches out to me. 'Darby, we're not

sending her home. Her mum's coming to pick her up! She was always going home today. And maybe it'll be good for Kaydee and Lissa to have some time apart. It's been a very intense weekend.'

'I don't want them apart,' I say obstinately. 'I want them together. And if you want Kaydee to be happy, then you should want that too.'

Dad says, 'It's up to them to decide if they'll stay together.'

'But you have to tell them it's OK,' I say. And suddenly I realise – this is The Thing. This is The Answer. 'You have to tell them, Dad. And Mum. You have to *say* you want them to be together. So they can be happy.'

'Darby . . .' says Mum.

'You're not listening to me!' I shout. 'This is *important*! You always say everyone's different and that that's good because we wouldn't want everyone to be the same. *I'm* different and you say people should love *me*. Well, Kaydee's different too. And you should love her. *All* of her. And that means loving Lissa too, because she loves Lissa so we should love Lissa.' I stop for a moment, because I've talked very fast and I'm not sure all my words have come out in the right order. 'Anyway,' I say, folding my arms and glaring at them, 'that's what I think.'

Mum and Dad don't say anything, so there's quite a long moment with no one talking. My feet feel cold and damp and I scrunch up my toes inside my slippers and feel a squelching. It's quite nice, so I do it a few more times.

Then Mum lets out a big sigh, and says, 'OK. You're right, Darby. You're right.'

I nod. 'I know.'

And Dad laughs and says, 'What would we do without you, eh?'

And I say, as usual, 'You'd be in a terrible mess.'

And then Mum steps forward and puts her arms around me, and Dad does the same, and I'm in a Darby sandwich, and I squelch my toes a bit more to make it all perfect.

Lissa is coming down the stairs with her case when we come in. Her eyes go big when she sees all three of us.

'Lissa,' says Mum, 'Paul and I need to have a word with Kaydee. Will you wait here with Darby for a minute?'

'My mum'll be here soon,' Lissa says.

I look at Mum, panicked. She mustn't go home!

'That's OK,' says Mum. 'We don't want you to go just yet though.' She smiles at Lissa. 'I'm sorry the weekend hasn't turned out quite as planned. We're hoping to do something about it.'

Mum and Dad go into the kitchen and through to the sitting room, and I hear the door shut.

Lissa looks at me. 'What does she mean? What's going on?'

'I am very brave,' I tell her. 'I am strong.' I lift up my arm. 'Feel my muscles.'

Lissa frowns. 'What are you talking about?'

'I am Super-Darby!' I tell her. 'I fix things!'

'Fix what?' asks Lissa.

'Fix you and Kaydee,' I say. 'So you can be happy again. It's all going to be OK.'

She starts shaking her head, and then I realise she's laughing. 'Oh, Darby,' she says. 'Oh, Darby, oh, Darby . . .'

I'm not sure why she's laughing and I feel a bit worried.

But then she looks at me and she says, 'I wish I had a sister like you.'

Chapter 35

When Mum and Dad come out of the sitting room, Mum's eyes are wet. Lissa and I are sitting on the bottom step and she's showing me a dance video from a TV show that I absolutely have to start watching.

Mum says, 'Lissa, we've been talking to Kaydee. Why don't you go in and see her?'

Lissa glances at me, and suddenly it's like there's something running through her, making her body kind of hum. It's hard to explain. It's like she's gone out of focus. I take off my glasses to clean them, and when I put them back on, she's gone and the sitting-room door is closed again.

Dad gives Mum a hug and then he hugs me and I'm thinking this may be the most hugs I've ever had in one day. The doorbell rings, and Mum says, 'That must be Lissa's mum.' No one from round here ever rings the front doorbell; they just come in the back.

Lissa's mum is small and dark and pointy all over. Her eyes are like Lissa's only more anxious. 'Hi there,' she says. 'Have I got the right place?'

'If you've come to pick up Lissa, yes,' says Dad. 'It's very nice to meet you. I'm Paul.'

'Beverley,' she says, shaking his hand.

'Got to get back to work,' Dad says, 'but you've got a cracking daughter there, by the way. Great girl.'

Beverley looks surprised but pleased. 'Oh – thank you.'

'Come on in,' Mum says. 'It's been quite an eventful weekend! Cup of tea?'

I sit with them in the kitchen, fidgeting. I am dying to know what's going on in the sitting room, but the door is still shut. Mum and Beverley make what people call 'small talk', which is very boring, and so I stop listening. Instead I just stare at the sitting-room door.

I am staring so hard that when it actually opens I jump about a mile off my chair in shock. Lissa sticks her head out. She looks *completely* different. She's all lit up and glowing. I know just by looking

221

at her that everything is OK, and I start smiling straight away. 'Mum!' says Lissa. 'I didn't hear you.' She comes into the kitchen. 'Darby, would you like to go in to see Kaydee?'

'YES,' I say probably far too loudly, and without even glancing behind me I run to the door, go through it and shut it behind me. I want to have my moment with my sister.

She's sitting up on the sofa with her bandaged ankle. And she's smiling at me.

'You are so beautiful,' I say in wonder. Because she is. I don't think I've ever seen her looking so beautiful.

She opens her arms and I crouch down next to the sofa and give her the biggest hug ever. 'Thank you,' Kaydee whispers into my ear. 'Thank you.'

I thought we'd say more than that, but it turns out that 'thank you' is enough.

Chapter 36

Sometimes things happen that are BIG. It kind of feels like we had two storms at the same time that weekend: one on the farm, one in our family. The broken greenhouse will cost a lot of money. Mum and Dad are still worried and spend every evening looking at bank statements and bills. But the fruit pickers have arrived for the summer, so I think maybe it'll be OK, for now anyway.

Kaydee is great. Her ankle is still sore but she doesn't care because she's so happy. She and Lissa text all the time, and I don't mind because I'm happy too. I know that Kaydee loving Lissa won't take her away from me. And that I was wrong about Lissa; she wishes she had a sister like me, so she can't be too bad.

Olly has started going out with a girl from school,

and although it's hard to tell exactly, I think maybe he's happy.

Bramble, Marmite and Pike are happy because Mum left the fridge door open by mistake last night and they helped themselves to the leftover chicken and the strawberry pudding.

I am not happy about the loss of the strawberry pudding. But overall I am fine. I even found Georgie, trapped between my bed frame and my wall, where she must have fallen while I was asleep. So I didn't need to go looking for Kaydee that night at all. But it was a good thing I did.

Storms can be scary. The outside ones and the inside ones. But every day now there is a big bowl of fresh strawberries on the kitchen table. And Mum has promised to do another chocolate hunt just as soon as Kaydee's ankle is better.

I've put the baskets under my bed, ready.

Acknowledgements

This book required a lot of research into the particularities of Down's syndrome, and I am very grateful to the following people who gave up their time to talk to me or to read an early draft: Colette Lloyd, Rachel Johnson and her daughter Emma, Alex Rigler and Ayesha Mahmud. Thanks also to Sally Phillips for her excellent and thought-provoking BBC documentary *A World Without Down's Syndrome?* Sally, along with Kate Jones and Marian Simon from the Down's Syndrome Association, suggested very useful places to start my research.

It's tricky to know what goes on inside someone's else's head, and if that person has Down's syndrome, it's even trickier. I've had to take artistic liberties with Darby's inner voice, and so any inconsistencies or inaccuracies in the portrayal of Down's syndrome are entirely my own.

Thanks to Kathryn Evans, who not only writes wonderful children's books but also happens to run a fruit farm on the south coast. I had an extremely useful visit there, learning about polytunnels and ventilation systems, and again, any errors in the farming jargon are purely my own. Kathryn's cat Pike is immortalised in the book (and on the cover!) as a thank you.

Thanks to Milly Weaver for bidding in the Authors For Refugees auction. Milly won the auction and thus the chance to name one of the characters after her very own Olly! I granted her a minor role as Darby's aunt too. Beverley Humphrey, who narrowly lost the auction, turns up in the book as Lissa's mum.

At Piccadilly Press thanks are due to a large team of hard-working people, but particularly Felicity Johnston, Talya Baker, Tina Mories and Ruth Logan, as well as the fantastic Design Department for another gorgeous cover.

Finally, thanks to my family and friends, who put up with my strange out-of-the-blue questions and are my solid support network in this crazy but wonderful job.

Jo Cotterill has had several careers – actor, musician, teacher, newspaper seller – but is now a full-time writer in Oxfordshire. She loves writing for all ages and has published over thirty books. Jo loves going into schools and talking about books and reading, and can be found making cards and writing music when she's not spending time with her husband and two young daughters. Find her online: jocotterill.com / @jocotterillbook

Down's Syndrome Association
A Registered Charity No. 1061474

Who we are and the way our bodies work is shaped by our DNA and by the experiences we have throughout our lives. In human DNA, our cells usually contain 23 pairs of chromosomes, linked together like a twisty ladder. A person with Down's syndrome has an extra copy of chromosome number 21. This means that Down's syndrome is a 'genetic condition', not an illness.

Having an extra chromosome means that people with Down's syndrome may experience particular challenges, like difficulty learning at the same speed as others. They may have hearing or sight problems, or may be more likely to have some other health conditions.

However, it's very important to remember that people with Down's syndrome are basically just like other people. They laugh and play and get cross and have worries and joy, just like we all do. If sometimes they see the world in a different way, that's a good thing. Because the world isn't fixed, and people aren't fixed, and everyone deserves the chance to be listened to and supported and loved. Differences are really very small. At heart, we're all human.

For more information about Down's syndrome, check out www.downs-syndrome.org.uk

Jo Cotterill and Piccadilly Press are proud to support the work of EmpathyLab.

'Today's world frightens many of us. Divisions are wider and stronger than ever. If we can empower the next generation to see and feel what others see and feel, we will be building a better future for everyone. In a big, scary world, EmpathyLab is a light of positivity.' Jo Cotterill

EmpathyLab is a new organisation. We are passionate about the power of stories to build empathy and the power of empathy to make the world a better place.

Working directly with pioneer schools, we are trialling an empathy literature and social action programme for 4–11 year olds. We aim to make a real difference to thousands of children's lives, story by story.

If you want to find out more about us, and read the astonishing results of our first year of pioneer work, go to www.empathylab.uk or follow us on Twitter @EmpathyLabUK.

Don't miss Jo Cotterill's previous novel,
A Library of Lemons – a story of a family
lost in books.

Calypso usually keeps her head buried in a book,
especially since her mum died – but when a new
girl joins her class who also loves reading and
writing stories, it sparks a close and special friendship. Mae's home is busy, lovely and noisy, just like
her – and Calypso loves spending time there.

Will Calypso be able to rewrite her broken
family and find their happy ending?

Here's what everyone's been saying:

'A story of great warmth and emotional wisdom'
Linda Newbery

'Beautifully written tale of dealing with grief
through the magic of reading and friendship.
Laden with literary references – especially *Anne
of Green Gables*.' *The Bookseller*

'A gorgeously written and profound story about
books, grief and friendship. Perfect for ten-year-
olds who've devoured all the Jacqueline Wilson
books and need to move on.' *Guardian*

'This book is absolutely spot on. Jo Cotterill is a
very talented author.' *National Geographic Kids
Magazine*

'This was one of those books where after
finishing I just had to sit quietly for a little
while, to process everything that I had just read
and to emotionally detach from the characters. It
is a really wonderful story, and I heartily
recommend it.' *Bookbag*

PRESS

Thank you for choosing a Piccadilly Press book.

If you would like to know more about our authors, our books or if you'd just like to know what we're up to, you can find us online.

www.piccadillypress.co.uk

You can also find us on:

We hope to see you soon!